Other Books by Lewis Warsh

Poetry

The Suicide Rates (1967)
Highjacking (1968)
Moving Through Air (1968)
Chicago, with Tom Clark (1969)
Dreaming As One (1971)
Long Distance (1971)
Immediate Surrounding (1974)
Today (1974)
Blue Heaven (1977)
Hives (1978)
Methods of Birth Control (1983)
The Corset (1986)
Information from the Surface of Venus (1987)
Avenue of Escape (1995)
Private Agenda, with Pamela Lawton (1996)
The Origin of the World (2001)
Debtor's Prison, with Julie Harrison (2001)

Fiction

Agnes & Sally (1984)
A Free Man (1991)
Money Under the Table (1997)
Touch of the Whip (2001)

Autobiography

Part of My History (1972)
The Maharajah's Son (1978)
Bustin's Island '68 (1996)

Translation

Night of Loveless Nights by Robert Desnos (1973)

Editor

The Angel Hair Anthology, with Anne Waldman (2001)

TED'S FAVORITE SKIRT

Lewis Warsh

SPUYTENDUYVIL

ISBN 1-881471-78-0
Cover by Max Warsh
Author photograph by Katt Lissard

Thanks to Alyssa Gorelick, Marie Warsh, Sophia Warsh, Bernadette Mayer and Wang Ping

Special thanks to Tod Thilleman

Spuyten Duyvil
PO Box 1852
Cathedral Station
NYC 10025
http://spuytenduyvil.net
1-800-886-5304

Library of Congress Cataloging-in-Publication Data

Warsh, Lewis.
Ted's favorite skirt / Lewis Warsh.
p.cm.
ISBN 1-881471-78-0
1. Teenage girls--Fiction. 2. Massachusetts--Fiction. I. Title.

PS3573.A782 T43 2001
813'.54--dc21

2001042056

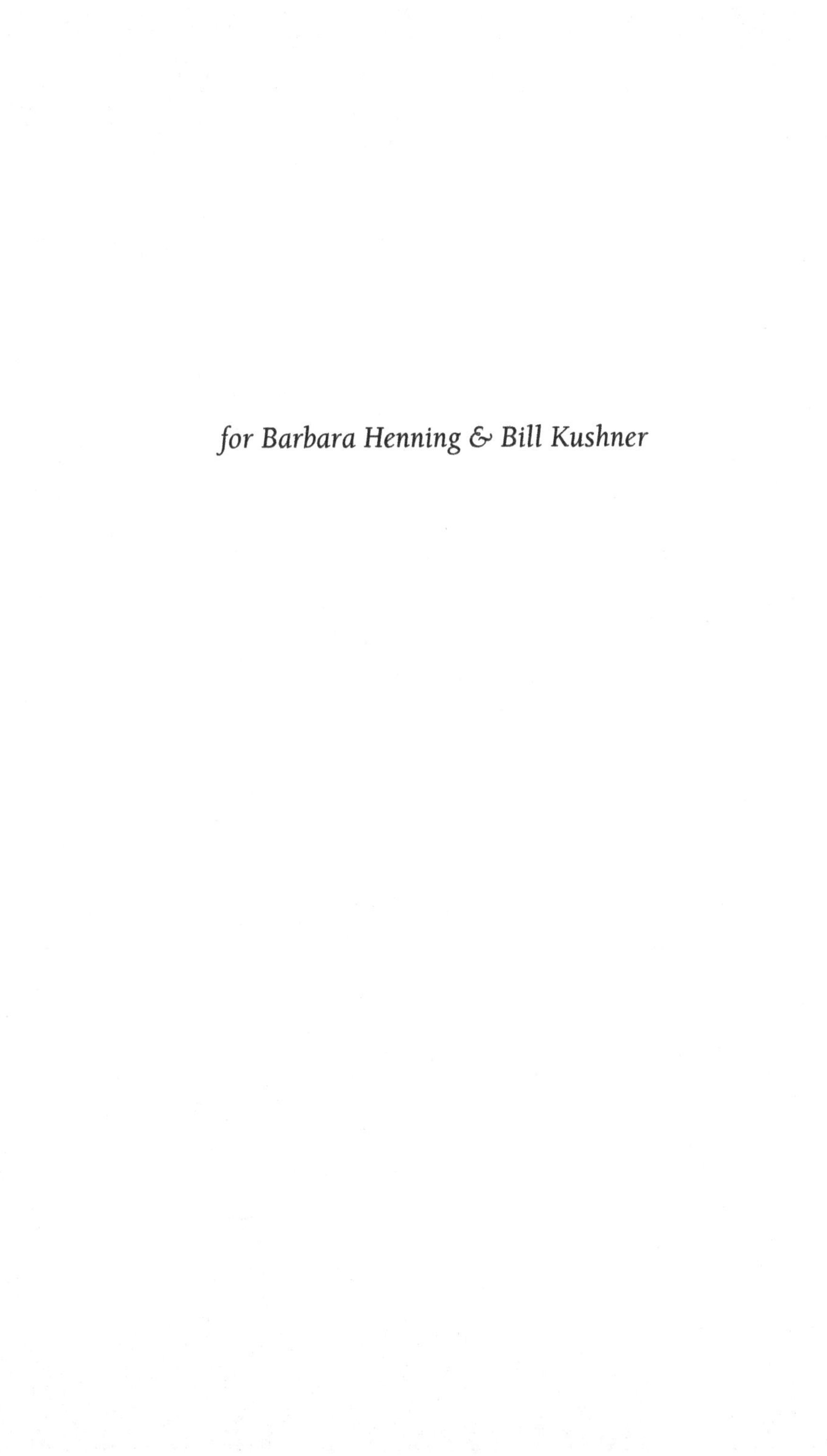

for Barbara Henning & Bill Kushner

Ted's favorite skirt was the color of sinsemilla. It resembled a meadow of flowers with a sprig of touch-me-nots hidden in the folds. Billie liked to wear it with a pastel-colored or awning-striped blouse and the lapis necklace her father bought her in New Mexico.

Sometimes she wore a sweater (a crewcut or V-neck, so the collars will show, but never a cardigan or turtle-neck) over the blouse. The skirt had no pockets. It zipped up the back, it swirled around Billie's ankles. The first time Ted and Billie made love he stopped her—"Don't take it off"—as she was about to remove the skirt and fold it neatly on the back of a chair. They made love on the Ryan's living room floor, a cushion from the sofa beneath her head, the skirt around her waist, her legs on Ted's shoulders.

"I like to make love with clothing on," he confessed afterwards.

Once when they made love he refused to kiss her.

"Is there anything wrong?" (Was he drunk?)

He liked to lie on the floor while she sat on top of him, the skirt caressing his legs and thighs.

"Sometimes when we make love," Billie complained forlornly to her friend Nicky, "he just lies there, his arms at his sides, and doesn't even touch me."

The skirt was a present from Joanne, Billie's father's second wife.

She bought it for Billie on her seventeenth birthday at The Lemon Tree, the most expensive clothing store in town. Billie and Ted had begun going out a few weeks before, but hadn't made love yet.

"He's the first guy I ever met," Billie told Joanne, "who even noticed what I was wearing."

She didn't know about Ted's predilection for making love fully dressed, but even if she had it's not something she would have mentioned to her stepmother. She tried on the skirt in the cubicle that served as a dressing room in the back of the store, behind the racks of clothing imported from New York and Boston, and stared at herself in the full-length mirror, smoothing the skirt over her hips.

"How do I look?"

She tried to see herself through Ted's eyes; no one's opinion mattered but his. As she zipped up the skirt she imagined making love to him—she knew it would happen, it was only a matter of days, of finding the right place and waiting for the right moment—the forest of ferns billowing over his legs as she climbed on top of him.

Billie was a senior at East Winston Regional High School. Ted, also a senior, was her third lover. Her first two, Arnie and Richard, didn't really count. It was just sex, that's all it was for them, another name to add to the list of girls they managed to seduce. Billie, only a sophomore at the time, had tried to pretend it was something more, but there was no escaping the fact that once they'd made love neither Arnie nor Richard had any interest in ever seeing her again. They'd gone off to college and two years later Billie couldn't even remember their last names.

Occasionally, in a dream, one of their faces floated disembodied into the frame of action, and then disappeared.

It was hard for her to admit that they'd always be shadowy presences in her history, much less that she once made love to them, and it mortified her to think that she might one day be called upon to recount her loss of virginity with a new lover—"I wish I'd saved myself for you."

Billie never questioned Ted about any of his old girlfriends and wasn't sure how she'd feel if she found out he was sleeping with someone else. His interest in making love only with clothing on made her think that he'd had so many lovers he wasn't interested in doing it in any ordinary way. They'd been going together for five months and as far as she knew he didn't have any other lovers. But who could be sure?

On their second date, this was a week or two before she bought the skirt, he began to comment on her clothing, her lack of makeup and overall indifference to the way she looked. He kept his tone casual so it didn't come out as criticism but rather as an observation by someone who knew what interested him, who had definite tastes about what a woman should wear.

His mother worked part-time in a local beauty salon and had indoctrinated him (at least this was Billie's theory) in the fine points of a woman's appearance.

Regardless, it was incongruous to hear the comments coming from him (he didn't take any particular care about the way he looked, why should she?) and Billie went home, after that first time, feeling bewildered and hurt. She wanted to please Ted but it was a matter of pride not to change so entirely to fit the needs of another person. Yet she wanted him to like her (if you didn't act feminine it meant you didn't care about men) and was frightened that if she didn't meet his expectations he'd eventually lose interest. Not long afterwards she wore the skirt for the first time, and pirouetted on the sidewalk ("How do I look?") for him to admire her.

Billie's mother, Chris, was amazed at the number of hours her daughter spent dealing with clothes and make-up. She didn't try to discourage her from becoming overly serious about one person (she'd been apprehensive that Billie would turn out to be the type of girl who spent all her time with her nose in a book), though part of her was also jealous of her daughter since what she herself craved was an admirer, a boyfriend, a lover—someone who'd take over her life to the point that she, too, might become inspired to spend all her free time pondering the way she looked.

She was still filled with anger and bitterness towards Mitch. She couldn't get over the fact that he'd left her for someone else (it was like a double wound that involved not only a perception of her own failure as a mate but as someone who was rejected, whose last ditch attempts to work things out, to "try again," had been spurned), and it was the vortex of all these feelings with their levels of contradictions, hate mixed with love, pain with the subtle memories of past pleasures, that made it hard for her to contemplate becoming that enmeshed with someone all over again. To fall in love ("whenever I sleep with someone I think about Mitch"), move to another city or town, and truly locate herself in the future: it wasn't impossible, people did it every day, but the more time that passed the more Chris doubted it was going to happen.

Billie lived with her mother during the week. On Saturday and Sunday nights she slept over at Mitch and Joanne's. There was a room in their house, with a slanted ceiling and barely enough space for a bed and desk, where she could go whenever she wanted. The desk was an old door painted white, propped on filing cabinets; the bed a fouton which doubled as a small sofa by day.

The arrangement of staying the weekends with her father was flexible depending on everyone's schedule and it was understood that she could sleep over more frequently if she desired. The room with the slanted ceiling was "her" room: that was how Mitch and Joanne referred to it.

Whenever Billie slept at her father's she woke feeling as if she were hiding out from the rest of the world. Joanne would bring her black coffee in a blue mug Sunday mornings and she'd lie in bed reading while a pink light spilled over her quilt.

Sleeping over at her father's gave her a feeling which combined the best aspects of safety and uncertainty. Chris's life was still in the process of changing—anything could happen: she was even talking about selling the house—while Mitch had already made his move. If she ever needed her father he'd come and get her, she could count on him to do that, drive the five miles from his house to her mother's through a blizzard in the dead of night. Chris's house was home, but her father's house was like a safety valve, the net suspended beneath the high wire to catch her when she fell.

Ted's parents were also divorced. His father, a traveling salesman for a company specializing in children's clothing, had taken his wares south when Ted was two and never came back, lured as much by the simplicity of living under a balmy expanse of blue sky for twelve months of the year as by the plethora of bored housewives he met on his daily rounds, one of whom he eventually courted and married, a woman whom Ted's own mother referred to as "that Dove woman," since that was her name. Ted associated his stepmother with the company that made the bar of soap and pictured her with "a glowing complexion," perched on a mountain top like the dove in the Bible who finds dry land. They lived with her kids from a previous marriage in St. Petersburg, Florida, and apparently Dove didn't mind that Ted's father was gone more than half the week, attending to the needs of other bored housewives up and down the Southern coast.

Every Christmas Ted's father flew north on business and called Ted from his hotel in Boston. Ted would join him there and they'd go to a Celtics game at the Boston Garden. They always had good seats, center court, a few rows back, and the close proximity allowed Ted to immerse himself in the game—these were his heroes, Bird, McHale, Parrish, literally in the flesh. No matter how involved he was with the game he couldn't forget that the man with the doorstep chin sitting at his side was his father only in the legal sense of the word and that seeing a person once a year entitled this stranger to nothing. ("How can I love him? I don't even know him.") Ted slept over at his father's hotel and returned to East Winston the next day.

"I always get sick right before I go to meet him," Ted once confessed to Billie—the fact that both their parents were divorced was one of the few things they had in common.

As Ted and his father parted at the bus stop in Boston, the strange man with the suitcase filled with bibs and pajamas handed Ted a legal-sized envelope containing a check for a hundred dollars. The two men stood at the bus stop in silence and when the bus arrived they shook hands—"I don't think my father's ever kissed me"—and said goodbye.

Ted was starting forward for the East Winston Regional basketball team. He's been a starter since his sophomore year. Billie, five feet nine, played guard for the woman's team. When Ted told Billie about meeting his father in Boston she thought of the play *Death of A Salesman* by Arthur Miller which she'd read in Mr. Luria's English class in her junior year. She wondered whether Ted's father had a lover in Boston, like Willie Loman, or whether (when Ted was asleep) he brought a prostitute to his room.

Billie and Ted met for the first time in the tutoring hall at East Winston Regional. (She knew him by sight and had seen him play but they'd never spoken to one another.) Billie was on the tutoring squad and Ted was failing English. If he failed he'd be suspended from the team, and the coach, not wanting to lose one of his best players, had suggested he get some help. They sat side by side at a long wooden desk, behind the door of a cubicle, and Billie gave Ted a list of books to read.

"I want you to read one book a week and write a 2-page report. Just tell me what you think."

"What I think about what?"

Ted resented the whole idea that he needed help. Playing basketball had become less of a pleasure during the last year and if he was suspended from the team, which he couldn't imagine happening whether he failed English or not, it would be the team's loss, not his. At one point he'd been touted as an all-state candidate, with the further possibility (the bait at the end of the line) of receiving a basketball scholarship to the state university. To the chagrin of his coach, his mother, and most of his other teachers, he made it clear that he had no intention of spending four more years filling his head with "a lot of useless crap," not when it was possible to go out and earn a living—even a job paying minimum wage was better than the charade of pretending you were learning something with the ostensible purpose of "getting ahead" in the world.

He knew he wasn't good enough to play professionally and the glamour of college basketball held no particular enticement. His strength as a player was his ability to detect and take advantage of the subtle lapse of attention in the person defending him, but this ability to pick up on nuances and tiny details and focus on them at the expense of seeing the big picture, the way life proceeded from one moment to the next to create a spiderweb pattern which was translatable back into life itself, worked against him when he left the court.

As Billie told him what she expected of him he noticed that the middle button of her blouse was open and as she bent towards him he caught a glimpse of her black bra.

Mitch taught English at the local community college in Pittsfield, and had helped Billie prepare the list. *The Sun Also Rises*, *The Stranger*, *Madame Bovary*, *Great Expectations*, *Tender is the Night*.

"There should be more American writers on the list," Joanne had said, looking over their shoulders.

Joanne, who taught composition at the same college as Mitch, that's where they'd met, was writing her dissertation on the concept of "breathlessness" (or "loss of breath") in the stories of Edgar Allen Poe, concentrating on the stories that related to Poe's mother, Elizabeth, who died of pneumonia in Richmond, Virginia when Poe was three years old. She suggested that Billie start Ted off with an anthology of short stories: Poe, Hawthorne,

Faulkner—she pulled a book down from the shelf—but Billie argued that the novels would give them more to talk about, and that there was something wrong with Ted if he couldn't get through a 300-page book in a week. A five page story, however profound, was too easy.

Billie described Ted to Mitch and Joanne as a "dumb jock," but that was before she got to know him. She reread all the books on the list and even read books about them, which she borrowed from her father, so she could answer any of Ted's questions.

They met once a week in the tutoring hall with its high windows and semi-private cubicles, the spring light cutting geometric clefts across the walls and ceilings. It was a form of punishment to be here, after school was over and you could be outside, and by the second session Billie wondered if Joanne hadn't been right and that maybe she was being a bit too hard on Ted. One story a week, two at the most, would be sufficient.

At the second session Billie wore a red sleeveless low cut jumper, and no bra, it was one of the first warm days of spring, and when the hour was up, Ted, almost as a non sequitur and with no previous indication that he'd been intending to pose the question, asked her whether she'd go out with him on Friday night.

"Where to?" Billie answered, taken by surprise: she'd hardly gone out with anyone since her fling with Arnie and Richard.

She realized that all the time she'd been talking to him about the novels he'd been staring directly into her eyes, not flinching or looking away shyly or embarrassed as most people do when it's obvious that the person you're talking to knows more than you do. She stared down at the words on the yellow legal pad on her lap, her notes for *The Sun Also Rises*, confused at the speed with which she and Ted had reversed roles; if anything, it was she who felt shy and embarrassed. She saw a list of names: Jake, Robert, Brett. She ripped a clean sheet from the back of the pad and wrote down her phone number.

Ted slouched in his chair, tilted back, and put his feet on the desk. Billie was tempted to tell him to "sit up" but checked herself. He was six three, with straight blond hair, a blond moustache, clear skin.

He'd put on twenty pounds over the last year but was still relatively thin for his height. During the basketball season he kept his hair cut short but during the summer let it grow out so that by the end of August it was long enough to tie in a ponytail.

In twenty years, if he continued to drink as much beer as he drank now, he'd wake to find a vague outline of his youthful self staring back at him from the contours of his bedroom mirror. He'd be nothing but a shape, no form at all, a man on a stool at the end of a bar in a country tavern mumbling into his drink.

His eyes were blue and watery: when Billie stared back at him she felt like she was falling from a rocky ledge into a quarry, where the reflections of the sky and the tops of the trees pointed straight down, and where someone who didn't swim well might vanish forever. If she stared at him any longer, meeting his gaze without answering his questions, she would disappear.

That night he called and they made plans to meet on Friday at seven. Ted wasn't the type who liked to talk just to hear the sound of his own voice (once they became lovers his unwillingness to communicate became even more pronounced) and after the arrangements were made he seemed anxious to get off the phone.

"I'll pick you up, Friday, at seven"—he must have repeated it ten times.

Billie had a few moments of doubt about whether she was making the right decision.

She put down the phone, rested her chin in the palm of her hand, and stared at a photo of herself, age nine or ten, which was tacked on the door of her cup board. She was sitting in a rowboat on the lake where she and Chris and Mitch used to go for a few weeks every summer, looking over her shoulder at the camera as if she was puzzled that life should have progressed so relentlessly to this particular moment in time—"here I am sitting alive under the blue sky and that man behind the camera is my father"—much the same way, as Ted's voice echoed in her head, she couldn't believe that by saying "yes" to him she was starting something (this is the way things happen, after all) that she might look back on with regret.

Her main concern was that going out with him would somehow interfere with their work. Maybe he's just asking me out to sabotage his attempts at learning anything or maybe he thinks if he takes me out he won't have to write the reports?

She even had second thoughts about calling Nicky with the news—Nicky, to whom she told everything, and who would be insulted if she discovered Billie was holding something back, especially something as potentially earth shattering as a date with the star of the basketball team.

"Don't tell anyone, but...."

It was pointless to preface what she was going to say with such a condition. By tomorrow, half the school would know that she and Ted were going out.

Billie had a hard time concentrating on her school work. She was rereading *The Great Gatsby* (a paper was due next week). She would read a page only to realize she had no idea what was going on, that she'd lost the thread of the story—who was this guy Wilson, anyway? And Wilson's wife? Who was having an affair with whom?

Every page or two her eyes wandered from the book to the wall of her room where an oval of moonlight was slowly ascending from a point above her desk to the crevice where wall met ceiling, expanding outwards as if it were breathing a life of its own.

It had been awhile since she'd experienced the nervous glow of anticipation that came with going out with someone new and it frightened her to admit that Ted's interest—for whatever reason—could distract her from her school work.

"I have to stop thinking about him," she said to herself.

He was in control of her thoughts, like a virus, but part of her loved the eerie feeling of sickness that came from being enthralled.

When Ted arrived for their date he didn't come inside the house to meet Chris, but honked the horn of his blue Plymouth and waited, slouched in the front seat sipping a beer. He'd bought the car, a mid-seventies model, as a gift to himself after working at Ken's hardware ten hours a day the previous summer.

Billie emerged from the house wearing a faded denim skirt ("you're not going to wear that!" Chris had admonished) and an old baggy sweatshirt from the University of New Mexico where her father used to teach.

"I hated the way you looked that night," Ted told her—not the same night, but on a date later that summer.

He didn't bother to get out of the car to open the door for her, but gunned the motor impatiently as she walked around the front. He drove with a can of beer, Hamms, propped between his thighs. When he finished the beer he tossed the can into the backseat—Billie was thankful he didn't try to bend the can in an attempt to impress her—and asked Billie to hand him another, there was a scotch cooler squeezed under the dashboard. She pried open the lid of the can and watched the road disappear under the car, wondering if it was safe to drive with someone who was drinking. It was a situation both her parents had warned her against (for most of the high school kids in town drinking and driving was one of the few forms of excitement), and here she was in the front seat with her knees against the dashboard, her life in the hands of a drunk stranger, thinking that at any moment she might have to leap free as the car careened around a sharp curve or veered into a tree, or into the car in front.

(Until a year ago, Chris herself had been a heavy drinker, a vodka with her morning juice followed by a beer at lunch, cocktails when she returned home from work, wine with dinner, and Jack Daniels with more beer as the night wore on. Though she claimed that the divorce was the reason she drank so much, Billie knew she'd been drinking a lot when she and Mitch were together. According to Mitch—"but don't believe *him*"—her drinking problem was the main reason they had split up.)

Ted knew about a party, or so he said, though when she asked him "who's party?" he acted mysterious ("some guys"), as if her question was somehow inappropriate or if it just wasn't her place to ask. Billie was surprised that he wanted to spend their first date around other people: it seemed to her, driving along aimlessly, that this would be a good time for them to get to know one another, if getting to know her was, in fact, what Ted had in mind. After her experiences with Arnie and Richard she was wary of her own estimations about what anyone, especially men, might be thinking. Yet possibly going to a party and being around other people was the safest thing to do; at least it would eliminate the possibility of going to park somewhere and fooling around.

If she were more like Brett Ashley, the heroine of *The Sun Also Rises*, she might take the initiative and suggest they drive out to the lake—that's where she'd gone with Arnie on their first and only date. But Ted appeared more preoccupied with his beer and with talking about himself.

"Is my writing getting any better?" he demanded.

He'd written only one essay, on *The Sun Also Rises*, so it was still too soon to say whether he was improving. His idea of a sentence was to string together a few phrases with commas, one thought dissolving into another, sometimes with no punctuation at all. She wasn't going to tell him how bad his writing was; learning the truth might be too discouraging. Not only wouldn't he ever ask me out again (am I being insecure?) but he'd probably request a different tutor, fail English, quit the team.

They both liked basketball and their parents were divorced so it seemed that they might have a lot to talk about, but Ted, opening another beer, was reluctant to steer the conversation around to a subject you might categorize as "intimate." If we can't talk openly with one another, Billie reasoned, how can we dream of making love? That had been her mistake with Arnie and Richard. If she'd taken the time to try to get to know them she would have realized that they had no interest in her.

She could understand why her mother felt so wary about finding lovers: she'd been burned once and didn't want the same thing to happen, wanted to avoid all the old patterns, refused to allow herself to drift on the crest of some illusory wave only to be tossed back to shore like an old piece of wood, the mottled plank of a small yacht swept under in a storm.

Billie sometimes found herself in the odd position of encouraging her mother to go out. She hated to see her mother (who was in her late thirties, but looked younger) "wasting away," which is how Chris, who managed to retain a bit of humor about it all, described her state. It was hard to meet someone in a small town, especially when most of the people you knew were already married.

Chris occasionally queried Billie about where, if anywhere, and if she had her choice, she'd like to live. They played a game called "hypothesis," where you pretended you had the mobility and a reasonable amount of money to do almost anything. If Chris had her way, for instance, she'd move to Boston, sell the house and find a brownstone in the South End. She was looking ahead (and in this sense the game had a realistic edge since even the most hypothetical scenario contained a glimmer of what was really possible) to what would happen when Billie went off to college.

Billie was near the top of her class and could probably go to college anywhere. At least that was the message she was getting from her guidance counselor and teachers. Chris knew for certain that when Billie did go off to school there was no reason for her to continue living in East Winston. There was a sentimental reason—this had been her home, after all, for fifteen years, all her memories of Billie's childhood were connected to this particular place ("you used to leap off that tree stump into my arms, remember?")—but that wasn't enough to outweigh the necessity of making a clean break, despite the risks and hazards of stepping out into the unknown.

Chris worked as a teller for the East Winston Loan and Savings: checking people's balances, issuing food stamps, punching numbers into a computer—"Do you want this in twenties?" If nothing else, leaving the town would allow her the freedom to contemplate new ways of earning a living, as well as increasing her chances (or so one might assume) of finding a new mate. She was good at her job, good at remembering people's first names and putting them at their ease, but it was ultimately a dead end, demeaning, and she often returned home filled with rage at the thought of all the time she was wasting performing a task "anyone could do." All the faces of all the people she saw during the day flickered in her mind like a row of candles at the door to a cave. She wanted to shut that door but the faces intruded.

On good days, she could turn these tiny encounters with people into small occasions. She knew how to be warm without being flirtatious—though it was always tempting to cross that line—and without giving anyone the impression she was trying to seduce them. Before meeting Mitch she'd studied art history in college (she loved the paintings from the Italian Renaissance, all the madonnas with angelic faces hugging tiny babies to their breasts) but had long ago lost sight of her original dream.

Billie and Ted decided not to go to the party. To Billie's relief, parking at the lake wasn't even discussed. Instead, they went to The Willows, a small roadside bar dwarfed by an irregular half-circle of elms (the willow trees which gave the place its name had been cut down years ago), on the road from East Winston to Carmel. Ted assured her that they'd be allowed to drink even though they were underage.

"I know the bartender," he said, matter-of-factly, not trying to impress her but implying that going to The Willows was something he did frequently.

The bartender's name was Whip. That's what everyone called him because he had a scar on his right cheek extending from the corner of his eye to the corner of his mouth. His first wife—this was the rumor—had inflicted the damage, enraged because Whip had been having an affair with her best friend.

"How did you get the scar?"—Whip was sick of being asked that question. It was hard to live in the present, to look at yourself in the mirror every day, when your face was marked so indelibly by a sign of the past.

An enormous pair of antlers, notched in a round plaque of decayed wood, jutted out above the bar. Many of the bottles stacked in an irregular pyramid behind the bar were covered with dust or empty. Whip once told Ted that the owners of the bar were losing interest and thinking of selling it or moving it to a road where there was more traffic in order to take advantage of the influx of tourists during the summer. In its present state, except for the antlers, which Whip bragged were the largest antlers anywhere (though he wasn't responsible for their presence behind the bar, he was proud of them nonetheless, and would often invent stories about their origin, much the same way he'd make up stories about how he got the scar), there was no reason why anyone should make a special effort to visit The Willows.

Whip raised his eyebrows when he saw Ted and Billie walk through the door. Ted always came to the bar by himself and Whip (who'd just finished telling a guy in a toupée and a suit and tie that he'd received the scar in a knife fight with a sailor on a dark street in Liverpool) was beginning to wonder whether the kid had any girlfriends.

"Do you come here often?" Billie asked, once they were seated in a booth.

The bar was crowded with middle-aged men in work shirts and baseball caps, and Billie had the impression that everyone was staring at her, sizing her up over the rims of their shot glasses. She didn't particularly like beer but let Ted order one for her. Whip was in his late thirties, the same age as Chris, and it occurred to Billie that they might make a good pair.

"Is he married?"

"Who?"

"The bartender."

"Why," sullen, not looking at her, wiping his mouth with the back of his hand, "you interested?"

He finished his beer and ordered another before Billie even started her first.

"What does your father do?" she said, trying to make conversation.

But he didn't answer and she began to feel like it was time to go home.

"Isn't there anything you want to talk about?"

The jukebox was stacked with old country and western numbers; as she asked the question, Webb Pierce's "Satisfied Mind" was buzzing in her ears. She watched Ted openly admire the only other woman in the bar, a platinum blonde in tight jeans and a white sleeveless jersey. She sat on a stool, spinning around expectantly when anyone new entered the bar, a recent divorcee whose husband had left her for a younger woman and whose children were now old enough to stay home alone.

"I should tell my mother about this place," Billie thought, realizing that Chris probably knew about The Willows all too well and that she was probably better off not even mentioning that she'd come here with Ted.

When they left the bar Ted insisted on driving her home, even though he was drunk and almost fell down as he opened the car door. When Billie suggested that she drive he pretended not to hear. It hadn't been much of a date, but they'd managed to touch upon family intrigues and basketball, as well as all the books on the list: he was presently reading *The Stranger*. Already, Billie began framing in her mind a possible ultimatum: I won't go out with you again unless you stop drinking. But just having this thought made her wonder whether she was being too hard on him.

"Do you want to kiss me?" she asked when they were parked outside her house.

A kiss was his reward for getting her home safely. She was confident that he wouldn't abuse her overture and assume that her offer of a kiss meant she wanted to make love or that she was leading him to the point where he might attempt to undress her, drunkenly, that that's what she wanted. It wasn't unusual for a woman to make the first move, but the gesture was lost on Ted; he leaned forward, moaned, tilted his head against the steering wheel.

"Why don't you come in for awhile and have some coffee?"

There was a light on in the upstairs bedroom which meant that Chris (it was only a few minutes past midnight) was still awake. Reading the latest Ruth Rendell, in bed with a cup of tea. Her mother would come downstairs in her bathrobe and they'd all sit around the kitchen table and talk as if they'd known one another forever.

"I don't drink coffee," more coherent than Billie imagined it was possible to be after drinking eight beers. She'd made a mental note each time he finished one and tossed the can in the back seat and opened another. What she didn't know was how many he'd had before he picked her up.

"Can I see you again?" barely audible, as if making an effort to sound as pathetic as possible.

Billie had the feeling that if she said "no" he'd do something destructive, like total his car on the way home, and that his immediate safety was dependent on her response. She could always say "yes" and when he called later in the week, or when she saw him at school, she could tell him she'd changed her mind. It was unfair of him, she thought, to ask such a question at this moment. Neither Arnie nor Richard had even acknowledged her when they passed in the hallway at school a few days after making love to her, and here was Ted, who wouldn't even kiss her, asking whether they could go out on another date. She put her hand on his shoulder and pressed her lips to the side of his neck. She wanted to say "I'll see you Monday" or "drive carefully" or "I had a good time," but her heart was too full for words.

Annette Ryan's glass panelled medicine cabinet extended the length and width of one bathroom wall. Billie had never seen so much makeup in her life. She lifted each bottle, tube or jar off the shelves, turning them in her hands as if they were Mayan artifacts, examining the labels. Some of the jars had been left uncapped; a sickly mold surrounded the edges, the contents had evaporated. Billie couldn't believe anyone could be so careless. ("If you had as much money as Annette Ryan you could afford to be careless," Chris said when Billie described the clutter of the shelves.) Billie's own collection of makeup was small enough to fit into a large purse which she stuffed into one of the zippered compartments of her leather pocketbook.

Until she began seeing Ted, Billie always felt like she was being indulgent when she spent money on makeup. And on clothing as well. She didn't have much money to spend on anything and depended on other people to provide her with her accoutrements.

In the past, before the Ted era began, at the moment when she'd have to decide what to wear each morning before going to school, she'd throw up her hands at the thought that her appearance might matter to anyone. Why spend these precious moments spinning in circles in front of a mirror, discarding this skirt or that sweater in favor of another? Who really cared?

The point of makeup, perfume, jewelry and clothing was to enhance one's sexual attractiveness. (The word "cosmetic" is derived from the Greek word "kosmeo," which means to order, to harmonize.)

Presumably, it made a person feel better about herself as well. Billie couldn't remember what she was wearing the night she slept with Arnie and Richard. Not both of them on the same night, but on two different occasions, a week apart. She remembered spreading the blanket over the sand. She remembered kneeling in the moonlight, fumbling with the belt of Arnie's pants. She remembered watching the moon disappear behind a fragment of cloud as Arnie, two inches shorter than Billie, maneuvered between her legs. It was over, it was almost over, he was breathing heavily now, he was gone forever.

Whenever anyone asked Billie what she wanted for her birthday, she'd rattle off the name brands—Revlon, Estee Lauder, Cover Girl—as if she were listing the characters (Pip, Joe Gargery, Mrs. Haversham) in a Dickens novel. In the past, she hadn't cared whether anyone was attracted to her. After her experiences with Arnie and Richard she'd decided to give up on men; it was hard to think of them as "men" but they weren't "boys" either. Whenever anyone referred to her as a "girl" she felt slighted. Yet she didn't feel like a woman, not in the usual sense. Chris and Joanne were women. She was a "teenager," sure, but that term sounded like something someone invented to fit a category of persons who couldn't otherwise be defined. It didn't seem right.

On rainy Sunday mornings, at Mitch and Joanne's, when she didn't feel like lying in bed reading, she went to the bathroom and painted her toenails bright orange or magenta, just to experiment. She'd take a long bath, shave her legs with a disposable razor, masturbate. In her favorite fantasy, she was sitting on the toilet when Ted came in to use the bathroom and ended up having an orgasm and peeing in her mouth at the same time. It made her crazy.

Makeup, clothing, perfume, jewelry—these were the main subjects of conversation among the other girls at school. Even Nicky, her best friend, seemed to have nothing else on her mind. The girls competed with one another, not so much to see who could attract the best looking boys (most of whom, except for Ted—and it was here that Ted differed from everyone else—were oblivious to the time and energy the girls took with their appearance) but to see who could develop the most distinctive look, even if it was only an imitation of the models in the fashion magazines which they studied furiously the same way the boys poured over their copies of *Penthouse* and *Hustler*.

Billie went out on a few dates during her junior year but refused to let the boys (alas, there was no way you could think of these guys as "men") kiss her good night. She never went out with anyone more than once.

She had the reputation of being a prude, an egomaniac, a supercilious bitch (these were the words the guys she went out with used to describe her when they talked about her among themselves) but Billie couldn't care less what anyone else thought.

She spent her junior year concentrating on school work and basketball. She had a small crush on Mr. Luria, the English teacher, who had two teenage daughters of his own, and she devoted herself to pleasing him. At night, lying in bed, she fantasized about what it might be like to make love to him, but always stopped short of the moment when they actually did it, preferring to concentrate on the more sedate image of herself and her teacher sitting on a couch together reading aloud from *Moby Dick* or *King Lear*. (Once, in Mr. Luria's classroom, she excused herself and went to the bathroom to masturbate. In her fantasy, she was walking home from school when he stopped her in his car and gave her a ride.)

She was still curious about sex. Nicky even gave her a copy of *The Joy of Sex* for Christmas (as a joke), but she had plenty of time to experiment—at least that's what Chris always reminded her.

"You have your whole life ahead of you"—if she heard that again she'd scream.

She told her mother that she lost her virginity, but only after a long period of time had elapsed, and only after she made the decision not to sleep with anyone else, or even go out on dates with anyone unless she felt the other person cared about her in a genuine way. It was up to her, she realized, to define "genuine" in a way that made sense to herself, and ignore the pressure to go out with anyone just for the sake of "going out."

And Ted was that person, or so she thought.

Some nights, instead of studying, she'd lie on her bed turning the pages of *Mademoiselle*, *Glamour*, *Vogue*. Most of the cosmetics in Annette Ryan's medicine cabinet were products she'd seen advertised on the glossy pages of the fashion magazines: Revlon midnight plum eye shadow, Coty face powder, Cover Girl oil control makeup, Estee Lauder skin cream, Clinique skin texture lotion, Vidal Sassoon protein moisturizer, Fabrege mousse, April facial scrub, Fresh musk after bath splash, Almay one coat mascara. She wondered how she could become a model, if there was any hope. She was tall enough but her breasts were too large.

"You have nice breasts," Ted once said—a rare compliment.

The bathroom was at the end of a hall on the second floor, adjacent to Howard and Annette Ryan's bedroom. Billie wanted to check out Annette's clothing (her closets, her bureau drawers) but the door of the bedroom was always locked. A locked door implied a secret: "They're perverts, I bet" was Nicky's theory, which for her meant a room full of whips, dildos and chains. Billie thought her friend might be right: most people in small towns don't even lock their front doors, don't anticipate crime the way people in cities do. If someone's raped or murdered in a small town it's a big deal, while city people don't think twice if they open the morning paper and the headline, in bold black letters, shoots out at them—HEADLESS BODY FOUND IN TOPLESS BAR—as they drink their coffee. If you walk down a badly lit street late at night, if you come home alone to an empty apartment or loft, if you ride up in an elevator by yourself after midnight, if you're the only person in a subway car—these are a few of the situations to avoid if you want to survive life in the city.

Some people, on the other hand, grow addicted to the feeling of fear, and court situations and places where violence is most likely to occur.

Once or twice a year Billie went to New York, usually with her father and his second wife, Joanne. Billie didn't like to think of Joanne as her "stepmother," though for the sake of accuracy, and for lack of any other word, that's who she was. Whenever she introduced Joanne to one of her friends she'd say: "This is my father's new old lady," though after a few years she realized she couldn't say "new" any more. Finally she hit upon the idea of introducing Joanne as "a friend of my father," though it was more than likely the person she was introducing her to knew that Joanne and Mitch were already married.

Chris occasionally questioned Billie about Joanne—what was she like? Do you like her more than me? Chris still considered Joanne her rival, even though she and Mitch had been divorced for five years.

Sometimes Billie let Chris put on her makeup. They sat facing one another in Chris's bedroom, Billie staring at her reflection in the oval mirror above the vanity, while her mother told her stories about how she and Mitch first met, what it had been like during those first years after Billie was born, "when we were happy," implying that the history of their marriage could be split into at least three phases: happiness, disintegration, and some kind of grand finale, which lasted for more than a year, both of them trying halfheartedly to hold their marriage together.

In the course of one of these conversations, which were more like monologues since Billie had a hard time getting in a few words edgewise and was ultimately stunned by her mother's openness (they had rarely talked this way before), Billie expressed the concern (common among the children of divorced parents) that she was the reason they split up.

Chris hedged, as if there was something about Billie's theory that might be true. Both she and Mitch had wanted children, and the period right after Billie was born had been the best time in their marriage. Chris wasn't about to tell her daughter (why disillusion her?) that Mitch wanted to have girlfriends, other lovers, that he fooled around even when she was pregnant, even though Chris had made it clear to him that she wasn't interested in a non-monogomous relationship ("if I ever slept with anyone Mitch would hit the ceiling").

Joanne wasn't the only woman Mitch had gone to bed with in the course of his marriage to Chris. He came home late from work, made up some excuse, but Chris knew—"don't ask me how I knew, I could read his mind"—that he'd been with someone else.

During these conversations, Billie realized the extent of her mother's loneliness: how rarely she went out, even with her few close women friends, how much time she spent by herself. All Billie had to do was ask a question about the past and the older woman's eyes lit up. Once she started talking about her life she couldn't stop.

It was nine o'clock and the Ryan twins, Emma and Sara, were asleep. Billie had just read them their favorite book, the one about all the exotic animals in the Bronx Zoo, a place where neither Billie nor the twins had ever been. She'd read them the same book practically every night since she began babysitting for them but the photograph of the crocodile with a splint in its jaw always got a big laugh. The twins had never seen a real crocodile before, much less an injured one.

"Zoos have animal doctors called veterinarians," the book said.

Billie explained the purpose of a veterinarian, hoping this information would bore them and they'd go to sleep early. Emma still had a problem about bed wetting and after she read the book Billie marched her into the bathroom and insisted she "do something" before going to sleep.

Often she tried—just to make Billie happy—but without much success.

"Emma wet her bed last night," Sara would often announce when Billie arrived for the evening.

There were times when Billie had the impression (not hard to believe, given the way their parents treated one another) that the twins just sat around in their innocent way inventing the meanest possible things to say.

Billie remembered the afternoon last June (she had been out in the driveway practicing her jump shot—Mitch had attached a hoop with a net to the side of the garage)—when Howard Ryan called and asked her if she wanted the job babysitting for Emma and Sara. Was she free Friday night?

"I got your name from Midge O'Brien"—Billie had sat for the O'Brien kids for almost a year.

It surprised her that a man would call to handle the babysitting arrangements, but Howard Ryan, as he introduced himself, didn't sound embarrassed or self-conscious about performing this task. Billie had been babysitting since her freshman year and this was the first time a man ever called.

"Oh God, not her," Chris said when Billie asked if she knew the Ryans, this guy who just called.

"But it wasn't her," she tried to explain.

She told Howard she'd come over Friday; he sounded pleased.

She and Ted were on the look out for a place where they could make love and Billie was assuming that a baby sitting job would afford them a few hours of relative privacy. She never asked the Ryans whether she could have guests and sometimes wondered what they'd think if they knew she and Ted fucked on their living room rug every Friday night. The twins were infatuated with her and it was a rare night that she couldn't bribe them into bed by nine.

She was good with kids, everyone said so, but she had a hard time imagining a point in the future when she'd have children of her own, couldn't picture herself in a house on a side street of a small town staring idly out the rain-streaked windows of her kitchen, elbows propped on a formica table top, chain smoking and reading Harlequin romances while her babies slept.

There was always the chance that one of the twins would come downstairs and discover them fucking or that the Ryans would come home early, but that never happened. Billie always double checked, after Ted arrived, to make sure the kids were asleep. It would have been fun, in some vicarious way, to fuck in the Ryans' own bed, so it was doubly disappointing that the bedroom door was always locked.

("What's she like?" Chris had asked after Billie's first night on the job and Billie had to admit that she didn't know, "she didn't say two words to me, her husband handled everything.")

Five months later, and little more than a flicker of recognition had passed between Billie and Annette.

"How much do we owe you?" Howard asked.

Billie noticed that his hair was thinning but that otherwise he was almost boyish. He had a resigned look in the depths of his eyes which signified he'd given up even the remote possibility that life could be better than it was or that he had the power to do something to make it better or different. The eyes said there was no hope left, "at least not for me." Billie had never seen Howard Ryan laugh, she couldn't imagine them (Howard, Annette) making love ("she's put the make on every guy in town," Chris told Billie), she assumed that at some point they had been different people than the people she was seeing, not only as individuals but in relation to one another as well.

She was curious to see the Ryan family albums. No doubt they were hidden away on the shelf or closet behind the bedroom door, in the same room with the whips. She'd spent hours studying her own family album, photos of herself as a baby, Mitch and Chris as lovers, newlyweds, proud parents. Who were these people, what were they feeling? How could everything change so radically, and in such a short time, so that the two people with their arms around each other in the photo couldn't even spend two minutes together in the same room?

Some nights, if Billie was in the kitchen when the Ryans returned (she usually went to the kitchen after Ted left: she was too restless to watch television and there was no reason why she couldn't stack the dinner dishes in the sink and sponge the crumbs from the counter even though she wasn't being paid to do any housework and it was doubtful that anyone would acknowledge her work), she wouldn't even see Annette. They returned home between midnight and one and Annette disappeared upstairs. It occurred to Billie that Howard and Annette probably didn't even share the same bed.

There was a small study on the other side of the kids' bedroom where Howard worked when he had to work at home, and this room contained a wide leather couch. If Ted wasn't so tall, Billie thought, we could make love there.

Howard paid Billie whatever sum she mentioned in response to the question ("How much...?") and drove her home, five miles. Home to the house which she shared with her mother, Chris, not to her father's house, which she also considered "home," on the other side of town, and where she'd sleep ("why are parents so stupid?") on Saturday.

She sat in the front seat of Howard Ryan's blue Cadillac and stared directly ahead through the tinted windshield, waiting for him to speak. The Cadillac didn't make any noise, certainly not in comparison to Ted's car, which took about ten minutes to warm up, even in the middle of summer.

Howard ("call me Howard") lit a menthol cigarette with the dashboard lighter and rolled down the window. He drove slowly past the motels and fast food restaurants on the strip leading out of town. Sometimes he hummed to himself and flicked the dials of the radio and tried to make conversation.

"What kind of music do you like?"

Billie was engrossed in thoughts about Ted, his drinking habits, the pained look in his eyes right before he came, but it was hard not to be aware of the man beside her as well, the hair on the wrist of the hand on the steering wheel, the gray sideburns, the wide forehead, the ripples of flesh on the side of his neck. And Howard, she knew, was aware of her: sometimes they'd catch each other staring and smile nervously.

"I hear you're a basketball player," he said on one trip, and talked about his own experiences (everyone likes to talk about themselves) on the swimming team in high school in Indiana where he grew up and where, apparently, he and Annette first met.

Billie was tempted to ask him the secret of the bedroom door and tried to picture him flailing a whip over Annette's outstretched body, though from what she could gather about their relationship it was more likely that she whipped him.

("Don't stay out too late," Annette once shouted down at them as she climbed the staircase after returning home, a kind of mock sweetness in her voice which embarrassed Billie. It was as if she were purposely, perversely, putting the thought into both their heads that since they were alone together they could do anything: stop off at The Willows for a drink, go to the beach and fuck on the sand.)

Howard was a lawyer. His office was on the second floor of the library in the center of town. Mostly, he handled divorces and taxes, an occasional case of breaking and entering. (There hadn't been a homicide in East Winston in twelve years, not since Yvonne Craig, Midge O'Brien's cousin, shot Bernice Donaldson, her husband's lover.) Most Fridays, when Billie arrived at the Ryan house at 7, Howard was waiting on the front porch, pacing nervously ("my wife will be right down"), his lips moving as if he were arguing with someone in his head. The twins were in the kitchen, Annette Ryan upstairs in her bathroom, a cigarette smoldering on the edge of the sink. Billie wondered if Annette's hostility towards her was based on jealousy or the thought that her husband might be attracted to a younger woman. Billie knew that Howard was attracted to her, but also sensed that he was probably too shy to try anything. She felt sorry for him, especially if what Chris said about Annette was true.

Billie couldn't imagine what it might feel like to be married to someone who slept with other people and who didn't even attempt to hide the fact as Annette obviously didn't. At the same time, she wasn't certain of the terms of faithfulness, or how, if one were married, one dealt with feelings of desire for other people (while making love to your husband or wife you could pretend you were in bed with someone else). Annette reminded Billie of the bad witch in the story she read to the twins before they went to sleep (the same witch in the same story her own mother had read to her when she was a child).

On the trip home, Billie sometimes felt a sense of camaraderie with Howard, as if they'd known one another forever and that it was no longer necessary to talk about what they were thinking or feeling.

"How could you ever marry someone like that?" she was tempted to ask, but never did.

Chris assured Billie that Annette acted hostile around all women and advised Billie not to take her coldness personally. And it was true: all the makeup in the world couldn't mask the sadness in Annette Ryan's eyes as she pushed open the door of her house ("she's a worse drunk than Ted") and stumbled upstairs.

In recent weeks, Billie had begun thinking about what her life would be like without Ted. She certainly had enough to occupy her time: she'd proved that to herself during her junior year when she rarely went out on a date with anyone ("why would anyone ask me out?" she'd ask Nicky, inviting encouragement on her friend's part) and spent weekend nights either practicing with the basketball team or babysitting for the O'Brien's or the Pignatelli's or Irma Blakely (a single parent, whose five year old son, Mark, refused to fall asleep unless she read the same *Curious George* book over and over again.)

Some weekend nights Billie joined Chris and her friend Barbara Ann, a woman in her mid-twenties who had already been married and divorced twice, in front of the television where they made fun of the characters in "Dallas" or "Dynasty," or watched them as they hennaed their hair, carefully packing it in mud and enclosing the strands under a tinfoil cap. Or she stayed over at Mitch and Joanne's, a quiet night reading and listening to Mozart and Vivaldi in front of the fireplace.

Some weekends she and Chris or she and Joanne traveled to Boston or New York and went to the Boston Fine Arts Museum or the Isabella Gardner Museum or the Met or to a special bookstore in search of a book which either Joanne or Mitch needed for their classes; at least going to these particular places was an excuse for taking the trip, for escaping.

"Every month or so I get the need to be somewhere else," is the way Joanne described her periodic impatience with small town life. For Billie, it was also a chance to walk around in a world where she didn't know anyone, to imagine what it would be like to live in such a place, to bathe in the exhaust from the millions of cars and buses, to be greeted at every street corner by a person with a sign around his or her neck—"I'm deaf, I'm blind, I'm unemployed, I'm a veteran"—a styrofoam cup in his or her outstretched hand. Though part of her grimaced at the thought of slipping back into the ease of self-containment, she'd begun to balance all the possible things she could do when she was alone with all the energy and time necessary to deal with her relationship with Ted, or a relationship with anyone.

"I'm sick of being in competition with a beer bottle," she told Nicky, who looked at her in a world weary way as if to say "What did you expect?" Better to be competing with a beer bottle than with another lover; one might as well count one's blessings in this respect.

But it wasn't only the constant beer drinking which made Billie think it was time to call it quits. When they made love, Ted refused to touch her. He'd lie on his back on the floor, his arms at his sides, while she moved on top of him, her skirt billowing over both their bodies.

Occasionally he'd kiss her breasts or put his hands on her hips under her skirt but most of the time he showed little interest in giving her pleasure.

The first thing he did after they finished fucking was reach for a beer or go to the icebox for a beer colder than the one he started before they began. Sometimes their lovemaking lasted no more than a few minutes; other times, depending on how much Ted had to drink, he could go on as long as a half hour. He had no apparent interest in being thought of as a person who was "good in bed"; his reputation as a lover wasn't high on his list of priorities. As a basketball star, he had no problem finding girls to sleep with; he had his choice among the most attractive girls at school, many of whom thought he was stuck up—at least that was the only reason they could give for his lack of interest in them.

Billie was the first person he'd slept with more than a few times and as a couple they were a source of gossip and consternation, not only among the other students but among the teachers as well, at least those teachers conscientious enough to take an interest in the personal lives of their students and who thought that Ted would be a bad influence on Billie, distract her from her studies, sabotage her attempts to get into a good college.

Some of her teachers thought that she had become inattentive in class since Ted entered her life, that she was going through the motions, that she sat in class with a watery look in her eyes—that she went to the bathroom too frequently and was often gone for ten or fifteen minutes. They compared notes in the teachers lunchroom where they ate their sandwiches and drank from thermoses of ice tea and no one talked about sex.

Sometimes it seemed like the skirt was a big flower or the leaf at the end of a branch of a tree and as they made love it was like being in a windstorm or the moment after the storm was over—manic blossoms of volcanic ash spewing white powder over their skin.

"Are the kids asleep?"

It was nine o'clock; Ted was on time for a change. He sat at the kitchen table with his feet propped on the seat of a wooden folding chair and stared at Billie, glassy-eyed, over the rim of his beer can. He could sense something was wrong. Whenever they made eye contact she looked away.

She'd been in bad moods before but this was different. "Different" was the word he used when he asked himself why he was going out with Billie and not someone else. It was because she was different that he'd been attracted to her in the first place, but that sense of difference could easily translate into "difficult," since there was never any sure way of knowing why she acted the way she did, whether when she said one thing she meant the opposite, or if her words ever truly defined what she was feeling. She might be disturbed by something her parents had said or by one of her teachers—"that jerk only gave me a B+"—or possibly she was upset at one of the characters in a book she'd just finished, outraged at the author for seducing her into his or her world and then rewarding her with a half-baked vision of what she already knew the world was like. She hated books that didn't have even the slightest trace of hope at the end, or where the person you were meant to sympathize with turned out to be a cynic or a witch, someone whose sense of self was based on his or her ability to manipulate other people's feelings.

Billie could be upset for hours or days about something she read in the newspaper: the death of 15,000 in an earthquake in Columbia, the plight of the homeless in Manhattan.

"Why is everything so shitty?"

She sat at her desk with her fists against her forehead, mesmerized by the thought that she had actually been born into this world and had to proceed as if all these things she read about didn't matter.

It was hard for Ted to keep up with her moods. He preferred to keep his life as simple as possible and until he met Billie had managed to screen out most of the horrors of the world. He rarely read the newspapers and when he did only the sports. If he couldn't see it, if he didn't know the people involved, then he didn't want to hear about it. He had his own life and his own problems and these people in South America and New York City didn't give a shit about him.

"Listen, Ted, we have something to talk about."

That was one way of beginning. Billie leaned against the side of the sink, averted her eyes and tried to stop herself from crying. If he had come into the house and kissed her, if he'd made even the most minimal show of affection, she might have forgotten her intention to end their relationship. She could always do it the next time they met, or the time after. The thought of never making love to him again was terrifying to her: even if he was an inattentive lover weren't there other things about him that made it worthwhile to stay together? If they really felt strongly about one another couldn't they find a way of working it out?

She would explain to him exactly what she wanted. She wouldn't get angry. I want you to stop drinking. I want you to touch me when we make love. I want you to kiss me when we meet. These weren't outrageous demands, were they?

She pictured herself sitting alone in the Ryan's kitchen on Friday nights without the feeling of anticipation which she experienced when she was waiting for Ted. But that feeling of longing was only an illusion, some ideal about the way she wanted things to be. And Ted was off on his own track, as always. He climbed the back steps, pushed open the screen door and went to the icebox—it was as if she wasn't there! She felt like pounding her fists against the wall or shattering a thin-stemmed wineglass on the kitchen floor: if she had a tantrum, maybe he'd give her his full attention. But the best he might do was ask her if anything was wrong, in that half-hearted imitation southern drawl which made him sound dumber than he was. Where did he learn it from, anyway—his father?

He had passed English with her help and now he could be the star basketball player for another year even though he claimed he didn't give a shit whether the team won or lost or whether the scouts who came to the games thought he was good enough to win a scholarship.

"Then what *do* you care about?"

That was their argument. Not sex, not basketball, not even making money. Money was useful, in Ted's eyes, if you wanted to get a specific thing, like the time he worked at Ken's Hardware one summer and after school to earn money to buy his car. He'd wanted a car so he went out and worked for it. (If you want something bad enough you can endure almost anything to get it.) He cared about his car but not as much as some other guys Billie knew who talked about nothing else and even read magazines featuring photographs of women in bikinis lounging on the hoods of 1950 reconditioned Chevrolets. Ted didn't care about his car as long as it worked.

All he wanted to do was lie back, like a retarded prince, and watch her lift her skirt over the tops of her thighs. He cared about what she wore, her makeup; when he stared at her, when he thought about her, he compared her to other girls he'd slept with, girls he knew he could sleep with if he wanted, if he wasn't committed to Billie. More than once he had assured her that he had no intention of sleeping with anyone else, that he would cut down on his beer consumption if it made her happy, that she was the only person in his life.

The last thing he wanted to do, as he sat in the Ryan's kitchen, was have a long conversation about what was wrong with their relationship. They had a tacit agreement not to talk about anything while they were at the Ryan's. On most Friday nights, she was waiting for him in the kitchen and within ten minutes they were rolling around together on the living room floor. She would unfasten his belt, lower his pants below his knees, and take his penis in her mouth. Then she would lift her skirt and lower herself onto him, hoping he wouldn't come immediately.

But this time was different.

"I think," she said, almost choking on the words, "we should stop seeing each other for awhile."

She stared at a circle of light on the black linoleum tiles between her feet, not believing what she had done. You can say something to yourself a million times but when you say it aloud it always sounds different, like someone else speaking, some understudy waiting in the wings for his or her big chance.

He was lifting his beer to his lips, he was swallowing, trying to look unconcerned: if he didn't respond maybe her words would just dissolve in space. The only reason they ever got together was because he was failing English and she was appointed his tutor but at this point he probably couldn't even remember the names of the books he'd read and written about during their tutoring sessions. His writing had improved—at least he no longer confused "they're" and "there" and "their"—and she would have passed him whether he'd become her lover or not. The fact that they became lovers had made her even more tyrannical when it came to their work. She wasn't going to pass him if he didn't get it right.

He hoisted his legs from the chair and leaned forward, playing with the zipper of his jacket.

"You mean you don't want to see me again? You want me to leave?"

She was wearing the skirt to please him, the green skirt with the flowers hidden behind the leaves, the skirt he often said was his "favorite"—not that she had an endless wardrobe of skirts or dresses to choose from, but for some reason he'd become fixed on this particular article of clothing.

He was like a young bull for whom the color of the cape is like a mirror; and Billie, like a matadora, stood across the room, hands on hips, untouchable, her long legs hidden behind the folds of the skirt which swirled around her like a veil, teasing him into submission. She was daring him to approach her: "If you come any closer I'll scream."

What Ted enjoyed most was driving around in his car, Billie at his side, one hand on the steering wheel, the other resting on her thigh. It was one of the few times when he didn't mind touching her. She lit a joint, passed it to him, and moved closer to him in the seat. Then she lifted her skirt, took his hand, and pressed it against her skin. Once, when she was really stoned, she opened his pants in the car and jerked him off as he drove. Instead of slowing down it made him drive faster but for once she wasn't afraid.

Some afternoons they'd return to his house after school. His mother was at work; they'd go upstairs to his room, turn on the radio. He liked to lie back on his bed and watch her dance to the music. She was a good dancer and took pleasure in her own movements, as if she was staring at herself in a mirror, watching someone else dance. It was a way of giving pleasure to Ted but it was also possible to forget that he was even there. She would hum along with the music, close her eyes, spin around like a gypsy, letting her mind go. It was one of the rare occasions when she could lose herself totally, even more so than when they were actually making love. Then, she had to concentrate on Ted, on his movements (or lack of them), on the absence of real pleasure. When she danced alone she had no one to depend on but herself.

It was true, her teachers were right: her relationship with Ted was driving her crazy. Distracting her from her work. All she thought about was clothing and makeup and ways of pleasing him. She spent all her energy devising strategies so that they could meet more frequently. Her mother worked from 9 to 3 so if they both took off from school they could make love in Billie's room....

"But doesn't your mother come home for lunch?"

She'd lie awake half the night imagining their future together, then walk through her school day like a zombie, hair askew, watching the minute hand of her Timex turn its slow circle past the Roman numerals which resembled soldiers standing guard over her fate.

It was as if life was now measured out in a series of anxious waves which flooded her heart and made her feel like she'd slipped through an invisible partition into a new dimension where time went by too slowly or too quickly and there were never enough moments in between classes or after school or on weekends, they both had to be somewhere else, always had other things to do. When her teachers called on her she stared at them blankly and asked them to repeat their questions, not caring if she was being rude.

In the past, she was always the first one to raise her hand: now, even on the best days, she could barely manage a vague response, a one word answer to a question that required thoughtful consideration. In the old days, before Ted, she always managed to say something. Now she was like everyone else, preoccupied with the way she looked, with the way Ted wanted her to look.

She would miss those afternoons in the half-light of Ted's room even more than their nights at the Ryan's.

"I think," she repeated, "we should stop seeing each other for awhile. We have to—."

There was no right way to say anything and as soon as she spoke she felt like she meant the opposite, that she was somehow out of touch with what she was really feeling. He looked so vulnerable, hunched over, withdrawing into himself, cutting her out, not wanting to hear what she was saying. He stood up and shuffled towards the door, the fluorescent circle on the ceiling catching the blond embers in his hair. Billie felt like a heavy cloth, soaked in ice water, had spread over her heart, that her heart was contracting, folding up, collapsing, growing smaller, till all that remained was a discarded bit of note paper on which the words "I loved you once" had been scrawled.

Alongside her sense of despair at the idea that she'd acted so definitively and in a way that was possibly irreversible she also felt the impulse to go over to him and put her arms around his shoulders, just like always, take his hand and lead him back into the living room, lift her skirt, lie down beside him on the rug.

"I'm sorry, I didn't mean it—you know how I am. You can do what you want with me—I'm yours."

But it was too late. She could hear his footsteps on the gravel path leading around the house. She steadied herself against the edge of the sink as the blood rushed from her head and listened to the sound of the engine of his car, the low insidious hum as he shifted gears and sped away.

The Ryans came home early, a few minutes before midnight, and for the first time since Billie began babysitting Annette Ryan didn't rush immediately to her room. In fact, she didn't even seem drunk. Maybe they'd heard that Billie entertained her boyfriend when she was babysitting and were returning early with the hope that they'd find them together in a compromising position.

"I caught you"—Billie could hear the contempt in Annette's voice.

And it's true, if Ted had stayed as late as he usually did there was a good chance that Howard and Annette would have found them together.

Instead, when they came in Billie was sitting alone on the sofa, watching the local news.

"What a nice skirt," Annette remarked as she wandered through the house, switching on the lights.

As always, Billie was amazed how thin she was, and how the clothing she chose to wear—a lavender ankle-length gown with two narrow straps over her bare shoulders, a string of white pearls cascading in the V between her breasts—accentuated her smallness. Just to be polite, Billie was tempted to compliment her in return, but the sight of this bird-like woman with hair frozen into a thousand red curls made it impossible for her to attempt a compliment without the risk of sounding insincere. So she said what she'd said a hundred times before to people for whom she babysat.

"Did you have a nice time?"

"I wouldn't call it 'nice,'" Annette said, perched on the arm of the sofa. "Everything's so fucking predictable around here."

She pulled her dress up above her knees and crossed her bare legs; as she reached towards the coffee table for a cigarette, the straps of her dress slipped down her shoulders. Her breasts were visible, except for the nipples, but she didn't seem to care.

"I mean in this town, if you go to dinner at someone's house once and then you go again, and the same people are there, there's the same food and the same wine and they sit you down next to the most boring person you've ever met and you have to spend the night listening to people talk about the fucking stock market, about Wall Street for gods sake, and sit there looking as if you're interested! As if you cared about how much money someone was making or who lost his fortune doing what. And by fortune you have to realize these people are talking about pennies and dimes; they don't even know what the word 'fortune' means. When my daddy used the word 'fortune,' when he had friends over for dinner, it meant something real. But these people? They make me sick."

As she said the word "sick" her whole body shuddered and her dress made lavender ripples along her stomach and thighs. Billie, who'd never heard so much as an "hello" and a "goodbye" from Annette, was dumbfounded by this sudden outburst, if that's what you could call it. She wanted to sympathize with Annette for the boredom of her social life but in a corner of her mind Billie kept thinking what her mother had said about her sleeping with other men.

"She comes on to everyone in town, even some of the high school kids," was the way Chris put it.

Maybe, for Annette, a boring night out meant going somewhere where there was no one to flirt with.

At the same time, Billie couldn't understand why anyone would want to sleep with her. You'd have to be pretty desperate, though maybe there were some men (or maybe all men were like this?) who couldn't say no to a woman who was willing to spread her legs.

How could Howard stand it?

"Howard, fix me a drink."

And to Billie: "Do you want something? A Coke? I suppose you have to go."

"Go?"

At first Billie didn't know what she was talking about. She was lost in her own world, remembering the night she and Ted went nude bathing at Lake Mansfield, the curve of his neck and the white tints in the center of his eyes, the sand sticking to her shoulders as he towered over her. It was one of the few times they made love with no clothes on and Billie had felt like she was drifting out of her body, riding a wave to the tops of the branches of the trees surrounding the lake then soaring through space like a comet, a cut-out figure of a person against a backdrop of stars.

Ted's eyes, when they made love, were impenetrable, iced over. Billie could never tell what he was thinking or what he was seeing when he stared at her and the thought that the person she was making love to was so far away from her made her close her own eyes, quick. If he didn't want to touch her that didn't necessarily mean he didn't desire her; but if he desired her (and this is what confused Billie the most) why didn't he want her to feel pleasure too? And she *was* feeling pleasure, she couldn't deny that, whether he touched her or not.

Maybe her desire to experience a feeling of oneness with another person was just something you read about in books. People, by definition, were separate entities, moving close to one another, then apart, and sex was one way of getting close, possibly the ultimate way. But if you thought about it too much, that part of one person's body actually enters another, it could drive you crazy. No matter how "together" you felt with another person you were still separate, no way around that, and when you died it was just yourself alone with all the memories of your old lovers.

And where were they now?

And what did all that closeness mean? And if you were ultimately alone, by definition, why make an attempt to get close?

Billie couldn't bear thinking about it. She was tired of wondering why Ted acted the way he did. If nothing else, breaking up with him would give her time to think about other things.

Howard stood at the entrance to the living room, drink in hand. He was wearing a black shirt with the collar points spread over the lapels of his jacket ("Why, Howard, you look positively flamboyant," Missy Dexter, the hostess of the dinner party they'd gone to, had exclaimed), the jacket cut tight around the shoulders, HR stitched on the pocket. The shirt had silver buttons, the pockets outlined with white thread, and Billie wondered if Howard was trying to pass himself off as a cowboy. Maybe that had been the motif of the party, or wherever they had been.

Annette, on the other hand, resembled neither a cowgirl or a rodeo queen, but looked like a hooker who showed up in the tent after the rodeo was over, a cowboy groupie who would do anything to get close to the sawdust and the sweat.

"Here's your drink."

He handed the glass to Annette who took it without looking at him, as if he was there for no other reason but to serve her, he was her slave ("Howard, there's not enough ice in this drink!") and when she asked him to do something he jumped to attention.

She was rambling on incoherently to Billie about small town life and how few things there were to do and how bored she was and how no wonder so many high school kids were killed in car accidents or committed suicide and if only she could convince Howard to move to New York. Billie felt embarrassed for Howard and couldn't understand why he let Annette treat him this way. She took her sweater, looped it around her neck, and started for the door.

"Howard, go after her." This was Annette again, shrill, out of control. "She's waiting for you to drive her home."

For a moment, Billie thought that this effusive version of Annette was going to try to kiss her good night, but as she started out the door with Howard she saw a glimpse of Annette's old self, cold and suspicious, as if a cloud with a dark crease were passing over her head, her face a shattered mirror of light and shadow.

"She's like a witch," Billie thought to herself, and as always she was tempted to ask Howard why he had ever married her. She tried to imagine them walking up the aisle of some church, Annette's white lace wedding gown trailing behind her, but it was an effort to picture Annette in such human circumstances. But then her own parents had been different people when they were married and look what happened to them.

Billie leaned forward and touched the dashboard with her fingertips. Unlike in Ted's car, with the cooler at her feet, she could actually cross her legs with room to spare.

"Your wife"—she didn't feel she knew Annette well enough to refer to her by her first name—"had a good time?"

"She always has a good time if there's enough to drink."

"But she didn't seem as if she had too much...."

"Well, Tab Dexter's brother was at dinner."

"Who's that?"

"You know the Dexters, don't you? He just opened that hair cutting place on Cliffwood Street. Well, it was his brother, Ray, who's here from Minnesota."

Billie wanted to pretend that she didn't understand what Howard was saying. She wanted to play dumb because the truth was too scary. The implication was that Annette had enjoyed herself because Tab Dexter's brother, Ray, had been at dinner. The scary part was that Howard seemed resigned to the fact that Annette slept around. Possibly she and this guy Ray were on the phone right now, making plans to meet the next afternoon.

"Was his wife there?"

"He's not married. He *was* married, I think, but I know he doesn't live with his family."

She caught him watching her and he caught her noticing. Then each stared at the other, openly, for a second, as a form of recognition that this had happened. Billie, aware that she wasn't thinking about Ted for the first time since he had left the Ryan's house, was conscious of Howard's awareness of her body. What he wanted, now that he had conveyed his interest in touching her, was a sense of reassurance that she wouldn't be insulted if he tried. But I do want him to touch me: it seemed insane that she couldn't turn to him and say, out right, that she wanted to sleep with him. Unfortunately, it was sometimes necessary to articulate one's desires (this was true for people who had lived together for years, as well as for strangers), and not take for granted that people assumed your feelings were compatible with theirs.

"Do you have a boyfriend?"

"I did," Billie said, curious how Howard would react if she told him about her relationship with Ted, "but we just broke up."

Billie shifted her body in his direction, sliding her knees onto the seat. She was wearing Ted's favorite skirt, but Ted didn't exist. Only a few months ago she had sat in Ted's car, under the tree in front of her mother's house, and kissed him for the first time. Now she was sitting here with someone else. She wondered if Howard cared about clothing, whether he would advise her about what to wear the way Ted tried to do. Annette was such a fanatic about the way she looked, but who knows whether she was dressing for his benefit. Usually Billie got out of the car and said good night as soon as Howard stopped in front of the house, but this time she lingered, wanting to make it clear that she liked being with him, despite their age difference, and that she could stay out as long as she wanted.

Possibly he thinks I'm just a kid, and that if he tries anything I'll call the police.

"You can kiss me if you like." It was up to her to give her consent before anything happened.

She spoke in the same tone she had used to tell Ted that she never wanted to see him again, with the same undercurrent of exhilaration at being able to put into words what she was feeling, and risk saying it. Yet when he turned to her and put his arm around her shoulder and maneuvered her head so that their lips could meet in the middle space between them, she felt less the pleasure of being kissed than the uneasy sensation that she'd done it all before. Howard's kiss was different from Ted's, people weren't interchangeable, but she still craved something more. It was here that her ability to articulate what she wanted deserted her.

She thought of Annette, locked behind the door of her bedroom, Ted sitting at some bar muttering into a glass of beer, Chris in her bed with a book and a cup of tea, Mitch and Joanne reading in front of the fire, Nicky asleep on her stomach with the covers scattered on the floor. Billie, whose own life was changing, wanted to be certain that everyone she knew stayed the same. She laughed to herself as she tried to imagine what they would say if they could see her now (Howard, still kissing her, and placed his hand down the front of her blouse, and was playing with her nipples) and what Annette would do if she found out.

But if Howard isn't thinking about his wife, why am I?

Billie woke the next morning feeling like a bridge had collapsed between herself and the outside world. She was on one side—and everyone else she knew was over there, on the other side of the moat, talking about her and pointing their fingers in her direction, inaccessible, out of reach. She wasn't certain who she was, who her friends were, whether her parents still loved her, nor why she had decided to end her relationship with Ted. All her reasons for ending it (his lack of affection, his drinking) seemed like figments of her imagination, problems she'd invented and blown out of proportion to make her life more complicated. Half the girls in school would do anything for a chance to go out with Ted; and here she was, letting him slip away. Why couldn't she be happy with what she had?

She had planned to spend the weekend at Mitch and Joanne's, just like always, but told her mother to phone Mitch and tell him she was too sick to come over. Chris canceled her own plans and spent the day at home.

"If you want to talk," she said, "I'll be downstairs."

Without going into detail, Billie made it clear that besides having her period, which had started that morning, something had gone awry between her and Ted.

"But I really love him," she burst out crying, admitting finally that she and Ted had split up.

No one knew their problems; she hadn't told anyone except Nicky about Ted's refusal to touch her. About his obsession with her clothing.

Everyone knew he drank too much, but Billie had never complained about it to her parents. There had been no indication of a crisis until she came home that night.

Both Mitch and Chris experienced a mixture of disappointment and relief. They had been happy that Billie was going out on a regular basis after spending most of her junior year alone. For this reason they were grateful to Ted without really liking him. At the same time, they hoped Billie wouldn't get overly infatuated with one person. If anything, they assumed that Ted would break up with her.

"She keeps saying," Chris told her ex-husband, "that it's like somebody died."

"Do you think we should send her to a shrink?"

It was Joanne, eight years of therapy behind her, who had made the suggestion, though the idea of sending Billie to some kind of doctor had come up once before, right after Mitch and Chris separated. At that time, both of them were too needy themselves and were hesitant about beginning a process that might, in the long run, only make things worse. They rationalized their decision by saying that going to a therapist was a way of emphasizing a problem that might not even exist, and how were they to know what Billie was really feeling. Of course she was unhappy; but it would be more a cause of concern if she weren't. Maybe if you ignore your problems they'll just go away?

Deciding to get help was something you did in the intensity of a moment where whatever one was feeling just seemed too hard to bear and where the feeling of pain somehow included the sense that the pain wasn't just going to recede or disappear over a period of time but that you had to do something to make it go away. And maybe going to see a doctor was one way of doing that.

Nicky tried to bolster Billie's confidence by telling her that there were plenty of other guys who were interested in her at school and that she could even arrange a date for Billie with her cousin Hank who was coming for an extended visit from California in a few weeks. Billie had met Hank before and the idea of seeing him again didn't exactly tempt her to jump out of bed (the idea of getting into bed with Nicky's cousin was unimaginable).

"She's just trying to help," Chris said, which surprised Billie since Chris never took Nicky's advice very seriously, and had once described her friend as "a piece of fluff"—someone who, among other things, would profess her undying love to one person one day and say the same thing to someone else the next without being aware that what she was conveying was her inability to love anyone except herself.

Billie decided to take a week off from school. She spent the first couple of days lying on her side, in bed, her cheek resting on her hands, a book open nearby, staring out the window. There was nothing to see except the top branches of the yellow poplar in the backyard and a patch of sky, facing west. It was very much what someone in prison might see looking between the bars of his or her cell and in many ways she felt like she was in jail except that she knew that she could get up and go outside whenever she pleased, that no one was keeping her imprisoned but herself. The blank space of the window was like an interior mirror which reflected all her feelings and memories about Ted.

In the course of an hour her mind leapt from subject to subject at half-minute intervals. Billie, who prided herself on her ability to concentrate on one thing for hours at a stretch, was horrified at the way her mind drifted in circles like an empty boat: no focus, no direction, no plan. One moment she was remembering the afternoon in the tutoring room, a few weeks after she and Ted had begun going out, when she let him put his hand between her legs (she could picture the whole room: the sunlight cutting smooth furrows of dust on the faded linoleum squares, the buzz of a fly in the shadows of the high ceiling, the voices of other students out the window—someone was revving the engine of a Harley and the sound rolled across the landscape like a thunderclap) and the way she felt like she was going to fly out of her chair as his fingers moved inside her; and the next minute she'd be remembering the scene in *Great Expectations* when Pip discovers the identity of his patron, not Miss Havisham but the convict he'd helped in the marshes when he lived with Joe and his sister and poor Biddy. She thought frequently of her former English teacher, Mr. Luria, and imagined meeting him outside the school one afternoon: he would take her hand and recite Shakespeare's 139th Sonnet to her as they walked chastely down a tree lined street, student and teacher, their fingertips and shoulders ("I wish he'd kiss me") innocently brushing against one another. She replayed whole conversations with Ted in an attempt to convince herself that she had tried to make it work, that what went wrong hadn't been entirely her own fault, that there was nothing more she could do.

"It was up to him to change, and he didn't."

Sometimes she carried on these conversations aloud, unaware that her words were audible, and Chris, though she couldn't hear everything, began to wonder whether her daughter was losing her mind.

"Can I get you anything?"

"No, mom, I'm O.K."

"Are you sure?"

Nicky called with the homework and to check in every evening after dinner and Helen Miller, the basketball coach, called every other day, concerned that Billie might miss too many practices. The season began in mid-November and expectations were high: four of the starters from last year's team were back and the fifth starter, Hannah Mulwork, was a transfer student from Seattle where she had been voted to the girl's all-city team at the end of her sophomore year. The coach knew that Billie and Ted had been seeing one another, and by now, since word had spread, she also knew they had split up, but Chris didn't tell the coach the real reason her daughter was sick.

There was a rumor at school that Billie had had an abortion. No one knew how the rumor started and Nicky didn't know what she could say to make people believe that it wasn't true except to swear, on behalf of her friend, that it was a lie, and that they should mind their fucking business. (The more you deny something the more people think you have something to hide.) It seemed like everyone wanted to believe that something more dramatic had happened than a case of the flu and her absence gave those students who were envious of Billie for her success as a student and athlete a chance to air their resentments.

Ted could be seen around school though he kept a low profile.

"Did you see him?" Billie asked her friend who lied rather than confess that they had passed each other in the hall but that he had lowered his eyes and pretended not to see her. Nicky always had a small crush on Ted and couldn't understand, no matter what happened between him and Billie, why he refused to say hello. The idea of being in bed with someone who didn't touch you had made her curious.

Billie sat in bed, pillow propped against the wall, a vase of tulips on her bedside table, and read a few pages of *Tender is the Night* while she sipped her coffee and listened to Chris getting ready for work.

Before leaving, Chris always came upstairs and asked her if she needed anything and reminded Billie to call her at the bank if she wanted to talk.

Some mornings, despite the black coffee, Billie drifted off to sleep again after her mother left the house, while other days she actually dressed and wandered downstairs, just for the exercise. She felt guilty about not keeping up with her school work, about not getting her body in shape for the start of the basketball season, but it was hard to circumvent the block of inertia which seemed to rise up between her and whatever she thought of doing. And she didn't feel like doing anything except lie in bed and think about Ted. Every time the phone rang she thought it might be him and though she wanted it to be him the idea of hearing his voice frightened her.

But it was never him: it was Chris, Mitch, Joanne, Helen Miller, Nicky.

"Do you need anything sweetheart?"

It was Mitch. He was going to drop in on his way home from work, was that O.K.?

She folded the skirt over a hanger and hung it up in the back of the closet next to Ted's favorite blouse, white silk with long tight narrow sleeves and a rip in the shoulder which had happened one night when she was going down on him in the backseat of his car. She'd never wear this clothing again. She'd retire the skirt, like the number on the uniform of a famous athlete, in Ted's memory. She loved the skirt: it was her favorite as well.

She sat in her room in her old University of New Mexico sweatshirt and a pair of jeans with big holes in both knees. She sat, fully clothed, at her desk, and tried to read. She read a poem by Edna St. Vincent Millay, the one beginning "What lips my lips have kissed." It was Billie's favorite poem, even though Mr. Luria had grimaced when she told him she liked Millay's poetry, as if to say: "You'll get over that." Reading Millay made her feel world weary and only increased her general state of exhaustion: there was nothing particularly uplifting about the thought that pain and suffering only increased as you grew older and that not even the most intelligent, most enlightened people knew how to avoid all the pitfalls, all the infinite little detours and back alleys, all the shadows where love became twisted and exploded like a hand grenade or burst into flames like a tinderbox shack on the edge of some big South American city like Rio de Janerio or Buenes Aires. All the convolutions of feelings were embroidered on the edge of an infinite spiral where fragments of memories blended with one another till everything blurred and it was hard to remember driving around with Ted without thinking of Howard and whether she should call up the Ryans and tell them she was quitting or babysit for them on Friday and pretend nothing had happened.

"How much do I owe you?" Howard would ask. She could hear his voice, just like always. She could remember his breath on her neck as he kissed her.

There was the skirt. She couldn't understand why Ted liked this one more than the others. More than the straight dark blue ankle-length skirt which buttoned down the back, for instance. Sometimes it made Billie sick to think that she and Ted had ever made love.

She sat downstairs and read an article in the previous day's newspaper about a private boarding school where seven "boys" (as the newspaper called them) were expelled after a complaint that a student had been raped. Apparently the incident began when one of the boys and the girl went into the woods and "drank a large quantity of vodka." They returned to their rooms for bed check; then the boy went to the girl's room where they "engaged in sexual intercourse." Then the boy took the girl, "dressed only in an unbuttoned shirt," back to his room where the other students made "insulting and demeaning suggestions." According to the article, no one knew whether the other six boys engaged in sexual intercourse with the girl. "I don't remember anything," she told school officials, who placed her in her parents' care.

Billie sat in bed, in her long red and white striped nightgown with the big bow at the neck, and listened while Mitch told her about his classes at Berkshire Community and brought her books: *Death in Venice*, *The Night of the Locust*, *The Idiot*. Billie was reluctant to admit to her father that she was having an impossible time concentrating; the only reason she was attempting to read *Tender is the Night* was because she'd read it already and knew it so well she could read it and think about other things simultaneously. So the books piled up, untouched.

Oddly enough, she and Ted had never made love in her room. It was safe here, in that sense; except for her clothing there was nothing to remind her of him, not even a momento, a piece of jewelry or a paperweight or a book. Occasionally she'd turn on the radio and hear a song that she connected with Ted (it was the same song she had danced to up in his room) and she'd lie back on the bed in a kind of swoon and relive the memory until it all became too much for her and she had to jump up and change the station. Ted's face loomed in every corner, larger than life.

By the middle of the week she began getting restless and decided, it was just past noon, to walk into town to the library. She didn't need any books to read but thought she might take out some back issues of *Mademoiselle* or *Vogue.* (Just because she'd broken up with Ted didn't mean she had to ignore her appearance.) She was secretly hoping she might meet Howard Ryan, who had his law offices on the second floor of the library, or at least put herself in the position where such an encounter might happen. As long as I stay in my room nothing's going to happen. It was a beautiful windy Autumn day, a fragment of a cloud floating off to the edge of the sky, the leaves falling one by one from the maples along the sidewalk. As she walked, Billie kicked out at the small wine-colored masses which hovered around the trunks like groups of people at a party. If someone asks me why I'm not in school I'll just say—*Oh, what does it matter.*

The library was on the town square, a colonial mansion with limestone columns dating from the late nineteenth century which the state had renovated so that it served both as library and historical monument.

Now it was supported mostly by private donations (some of the richest people in the state lived on the back roads of East Winston), a sizable budget which enabled it to acquire more recent books than most small town libraries. Billie had been going to the library at least once a week since she was a child and knew all the librarians by their first names (all except Georgette Fitzgerald, who had just been hired) and didn't doubt that all or any of them would question what she was doing in the library at that time of day if they didn't already know that she was sick. Possibly her appearance, if anyone noticed, would provide fuel for the town gossips ("Do you know who I saw today?") who thought she was suffering from something more serious than the flu.

She passed the desk for checking out books and wandered through the children's section, the reference area and the special music room where you could borrow records, passed Ms. Alper's office (it was noon and Susan Alper, the head librarian, was probably gone for lunch), till she reached the big reading room in the back. The room was lit by an ornate chandelier which dangled by a sinuous gold chain and by numerous standing lamps and by the natural light which skirted the curtains of the high windows which looked out on a large garden where in warm weather you could sit on black cast iron chairs until the light began to thread the tops of the elms shielding the west gate and Susan Alper or one of the other librarians ducked her head out the door of the garden and announced that the library was closing "in five minutes."

The walls were lined with books about art and architecture, this was the library's specialty, and in the center of the room long narrow tables held recent copies of at least a hundred different magazines and newspapers arranged in alphabetical order. In ever corner of the room there was a small table and an easy chair where you could sit for hours studying the collected architectural drawings of Mies van der Rohe or Frank Lloyd Wright. The library was almost always empty during the week, at least until school let out, and the only time it was ever crowded was during the summer months when the area was invaded with tourists.

"Remember me?"

Billie blushed. She hadn't seen him since the night at The Willows with Ted. Their first date.

"I even remember your name," he said.

"I didn't know you liked to read." Billie tried to sound flippant.

He closed the magazine, *Sports Illustrated*, and stood up.

"I don't. Want to go for a ride?"

"Where?"

"Nowhere, just out. It's beautiful out. Let's look at the leaves."

"You go first."

"What do you mean?"

"I don't want any of the librarians to see us leaving together."

"Oh shit," Whip said. "Do you really care what anyone thinks?"

He reached into the pocket of his jeans, pulled out a watch which was attached to his belt by a silver chain, and rubbed the scar on the side of his cheek with his thumb.

"I'll be out front," he said. "In the blue pick up."

Retracing her steps, Billie saw Gloria Fontana, her favorite librarian, standing behind the check-out desk. Gloria, who was younger than the other librarians, had moved to town a few years before from the Southwest, but no one really knew why she had come here.

Nicky, who knew almost everything about everyone in town, had once told Billie that Gloria shared an apartment with a woman named Michelle who worked in the town bakery, and that there was some talk (here were the gossips again, massing like vultures around their prey) that they were lovers. Someone had seen them holding hands; someone else, commenting on Gloria's short hair, said she looked more like a man than a woman.

Nicky herself had said: "They never have boyfriends. It's a bit odd, isn't it? Two women in their mid-twenties living together, no men around. What do you think?"

"Hi, Ms. Fontana," Billie said, there was no way to avoid her.

"Hi Hon," that's what she called everyone. "Taking the day off?"

They drove around the town square past the bank where her mother worked. Billie slouched in the front seat just in case she saw someone she knew. Then they drove out of town, through Carmel, along the back roads leading to a town called Manchester which consisted of a single general store with a gas pump out front, a post office, and a few dilapidated farms in the distance. Whip didn't stop until they reached a crossroads with an old fashioned arrow on which someone had hand printed the word *Savoy* pointing out towards the middle of nowhere.

"Where are we going?"

"We're just driving. Nice trees, huh? Pretty colors. Don't worry, I'm not going to kidnap you. I know exactly where we are. How's my old friend Ted?"

"I'm not seeing him anymore. We decided to break up. That night when I met you was our first date, if you didn't know. It just didn't work out. I may sound detached about it all, but I'm not. I really miss him."

"I haven't seen him much myself since that night so I wouldn't know what was going on between you two but I could have told you that it's hard to get along with someone who drinks as much as he does."

"Do you still work at the bar?"

"That place? Hold on tight." He veered suddenly onto a dirt road leading into the woods. "It's a short cut. No, I quit that job not long after the night you came in. In fact, I haven't been around here much since then. Just got back last week."

"Where do you live?"

He shrugged, as if the question wasn't relevant, and touched the scar with the tip of his thumb.

"Different places, with friends." He turned and winked at her.

"What did you think I was doing at the library, anyway?"

Billie missed the meaning of what he'd said. Was he waiting in the library because he had nowhere else to go? Was he meeting someone?

"I might stay around but I'm not sure. Can never be too sure about anything. It depends, first, on whether I can find work but what I'm thinking with winter coming on I'd like to go some place warm. Like Mexico, if I had the money. I was around here last winter and let me tell you I've been to Chicago in the winter, I've even been to Northern Michigan, and that's even further north than we are, but this place is the worst."

It was just a matter of time before she asked him about the scar.

"So you stopped seeing him. Or did he stop seeing you? Who's idea was it, if you don't mind my asking."

"It was my idea but sometimes I regret..."

"Listen, never regret anything. You had your reasons, right? Or did he do something that made you angry, did he fuck someone else? Or was it just his way of being that began to get on your nerves? It could be any or all these things, right? You don't have to live with someone every minute of every day to get sick of them. It's when you're able to see through people, when they become so transparent that you know why they do everything they do and their secret motives behind everything, that's when it usually begins to go wrong. I've been married myself, you know, and I've seen my own worst side as well. When you live with someone you have to go to extremes. Some people are able to compromise—live with someone they can't talk to but who provides emotional or financial security or something. But for me it's all or nothing."

They sat together on the patio of a place called The Hillside Restaurant on the outskirts of Savoy. The patio overlooked a large pond with yellow lilies floating in the weeds along the edge.

"I didn't know about this place," Billie said, happy to be out of doors. A tall, slender woman in a long white peasant dress, her hair in a braid, brought her a glass of white wine on a silver tray. "Who ever comes here?"

"That's a good question but I'm surprised you can't answer it yourself. The point is not many people do come here except those who know about it. In the summer, that's when they get their business, like every other restaurant around here. But they have to advertise because obviously no one's going to come here by accident." He nodded towards the road. "I mean you can count the number of cars that pass here each day."

I'm not going to ask about the scar....

Billie had little experience with men who weren't interested in sleeping with her and she realized as they sat on the patio and talked that she was secretly anticipating the moment when he would reach out, take her hand, and tell her how pretty she looked. She had wanted someone to talk to about Ted, someone who knew him, and that's why she had driven into the woods in Whip's pick up, even though she knew she was asking for trouble and if he did proposition her she had no one but herself to blame. But the longer they spent together it became obvious that he wasn't going to make a pass at her and the more tempting it was for Billie to reach over to him, take his hand, and suck at each of his fingers like she had seen someone do in the movies.

"Ted used to come to the bar and we used to talk," he said. "I tried to tell him not to drink so much but he wouldn't listen and when I told him I thought he needed help, that he was too young to be such a lush, he got angry. That's what people do when you warn them about a bad habit.

"They think that drinking's all right because it makes them feel good, less anxious about things if you know what I mean, but they don't realize that what it does is screw up your relationships with everybody. You can't feel anything, you get down on yourself, you think other people hate you, your sense of judgment is fucked up. You can never tell but it looks like that's the direction Ted's going."

He tilted back in his chair and smiled at her. His voice had a lilt, as if he were singing the line from a country and western song.

"And you sure don't know what love is anymore, you sure don't know."

Billie surprised her mother by saying that she wanted to babysit for the Ryans on Friday. After spending the week at home she explained that getting out for the night might be a good way of easing back into the world. What she didn't tell her mother was that she wanted to see Howard again; as the week progressed she had been thinking more about Howard, less about Ted.

She had thought about Whip, as well, but that was different; though she was attracted to him, she was willing to settle for friendship at this point.

"Call me any time," Whip had told her, giving her a whole list of numbers where he could be reached. "I mean I'm not just saying that. I mean it. Call me and we'll go for a ride."

Howard was waiting on the porch when she arrived, smoking a cigarette and staring out into the shadows.

"I tried to call you," he whispered, "but you're never home."

"That's crazy," she said. "I was home all week."

"Not so loud," Howard said, pointing his finger towards the roof of the porch, indicating the bathroom where Annette was putting on her makeup.

Billie took a step towards him and was about to put her hand on his arm, not caring whether Annette heard or saw them, but he eluded the gesture, muttered the word "later" under his breath, and went inside.

Unlike past Fridays, Billie made no big attempt to get the twins to bed early, and kept them up watching *Ghostbusters* on a VCR in the den. She sat with a big bowl of popcorn on her lap and a child on either side. The license to stay up late made them feel better about themselves; for once, they desisted from fighting and fell asleep in the middle of the movie. Billie carried each of them up to bed, propped their stuffed animals around their sleeping faces, and stood in the doorway listening to their breathing. It sounded like a soft wind, the hum of human machinery. Once she thought she heard footsteps on the path leading to the back door, but it was only a branch scraping a window. She went downstairs and dialed Ted's number but replaced the receiver, quick, before it even rang once.

She called Nicky but Nicky's mother informed her that her daughter was out on a date and Billie remembered Nicky telling her that she was going out with a guy named Bradford, a sophomore at Berkshire Community, the college where Mitch and Joanne worked. By the middle of her junior year in high school Nicky had decided that she would only go out with "older men" and refused to date any of the guys in her class. Nicky once told her that she let a guy do "everything but" on the first date and it was on the basis of his performance ("you don't have to fuck them to know what they're like") she decided whether she would ever see him again. If she decided to see him a second time that meant they were going to become lovers.

Billie cleared the dining room table, washed the dishes and stacked them on the drainboard, sponged the crumbs from the table, emptied an ashtray, rubbed the stains of tomato sauce from the top of the stove with an SOS pad, heated water for tea, found a tea-bag in the cupboard, watched the flame lick the bottom of the pot, took a potholder from a hook above the stove and poured the boiling water into the cup, carried the cup with the string dangling over the edge back to the living room, turned on the TV.

The living room was a mess too, but Billie was through being a maid. She didn't understand why they didn't hire someone, if they had so much money, to clean up the house at least once a week.

She read a few sentences from *Tender is the Night*, sipped her tea and watched the people on TV: about fifty couples, high school age, were dancing to a record by Madonna. The camera flitted from one couple to another, concentrating on their clothing, their hair, different parts of their bodies. As soon as the dancers realized that the camera was focused on them, their expressions changed: some of them began to dance with more intensity, kicking out their feet or spinning in a circle or passionately embracing, while others had a hard time suppressing a smile at the excitement of being on television.

Billie saw a skirt, worn by one of the girls, that resembled the skirt which Ted liked her to wear. She could hear his voice—"Keep your skirt on"—as they lay down on the living room floor. Until she met Ted she'd depended on herself to get through the day; now she realized how lost she felt without an object for her love.

"I like your pocketbook," she said to Annette.

The older woman slipped her yellow evening bag from around her shoulder, spilled the contents onto the top of the coffee table, and presented it to Billie.

"I think things ought to belong to the people who like them."

It was hard to resist, even though Billie had commented about the bag just to be polite, and would have kept her mouth shut if she thought that Annette was going to give it to her. She was beginning to think she preferred the "old" Annette, the person who stumbled home drunk and didn't even acknowledge that she, the babysitter, Billie, even existed. Until the week before, Billie wasn't even certain that Annette knew her name; all the arrangements were handled by Howard. If I told Annette that I liked her dress would she take that off and give it to me?

I think things ought to belong to the people who like them.

Billie wondered if Annette knew about her husband's interest in her and whether giving Billie the pocket book was a way of giving her permission to sleep with Howard.

Maybe everyone in town, including Chris, had misjudged Annette.

People were more complicated than anyone could ever imagine. So what if she slept around? Whose business was it anyway? If Howard didn't like it he could leave—such things happened every day.

"I wonder what he's getting out of it all," Nicky once said, after Billie described Howard and Annette's relationship, somehow implying that you had to be a complete lunatic to stay in a marriage without getting at least a modicum of satisfaction. Billie had read enough books to realize that it was impossible to truly know what went on between two other people.

One could take an educated guess, but who could know for sure? In most cases, what kept people together was mere inertia; easier to stick it out than risk making a change.

"I still love your mother," Mitch had once said to her, "but we can't live together. It would seem that if we loved one another we could do anything but it's not that simple."

But did that mean he loved Joanne less? Or more? If you were able to live comfortably with someone did that mean you loved them? Chris and Mitch had been able to live together successfully, at least for a while.

Maybe it was the way love changed through time—"I loved you once but you're a different person now"—that created all the problems.

Howard's work as a lawyer put him in contact with people who were unhappy living with one another for any number of reasons. They came to him when they wanted a divorce.

"It's usually the woman," he said, as they drove home. "For some reason, at least in my experience, women are unhappier than men."

Billie couldn't believe that there were so many people in the immediate environment who required a divorce lawyer. When she expressed this thought to Howard he had to admit that his business wasn't exactly booming and that in fact there were many hours of each day when he had nothing particular to do. The only way he was able to stay in business (the rent for his offices had tripled in the last year) was because of Annette's money.

"Her father was the number one hog rancher in Indiana," he said. "And when he died, when 'daddy' died, all the money went to his kids."

Billie felt at ease sitting beside him in the car. He parked under a tree just down the street from her house and when he put his arm around her and tried to kiss her she didn't resist. She would have been disappointed if he had just said good night without trying anything. She rested on the back of the seat and allowed him to move from his position behind the wheel so that he could press his weight against her. When they kissed he bit her tongue and the corners of her mouth but it was the type of pain that only added to the enjoyment. She thought of unfastening his belt and taking his penis in her mouth but thought it might shock him. She wondered if he had many lovers before meeting Annette. Until she kissed him the week before he seemed like the shy type but somehow that kiss gave him the confidence he'd lost during the years of marriage to a woman who acted indifferently when he attempted to make love to her and didn't hide the fact she was fucking other people.

Billie wasn't sure how far she wanted to go and was happy when he sat up and settled back beside her, his hand on her breasts inside her blouse.

"I want to see you during the week."

"Where?"

"I'll find a place."

"What will you tell Annette?"

Billie felt like she'd been rehearsing this simple sentence all week. Alone in her room, thinking of Ted until she couldn't bear it any longer, until she had used up all her energy thinking about this person who didn't care about her....

They had met at Indiana University. Howard was just out of the army, "but I'll tell you about that later." The stories would come later. Billie wanted to know more about Annette: was she really, as some people described her, "the town pump?" And how did Howard feel being married to a person with this reputation?

Billie didn't want to feel like she was interviewing him for the high school paper but in order to find out about someone it was sometimes necessary to ask questions—straight forward, direct, to the point—especially if the other person wasn't exactly forthcoming with information. Yet there'd be time for that. There was nothing wrong with sitting in the front seat of Howard's Cadillac, their arms around each other, staring through the windshield in silence, heads tilted back....

The house was completely dark which meant that Chris was in bed asleep. She trusted Billie and didn't wait up for her if she was late.

Billie could stay out all night if she wanted, as long as she called up and told Chris where she was going to sleep. It was Howard, in this case, who was restricted, who had to be home.

Billie thought of the two small girls, Emma and Sara, in their room upstairs, surrounded by their dolls and teddy bears. Emma slept on her stomach and kicked the blankets off the bed, just like Billie used to do, or so Chris had told her, when she was a kid.

A car was coming towards them, headlights leveling a path through the mist, and Billie felt the temptation to duck down in the seat just in case it was someone she knew. She realized that it was just a matter of time before somebody found out that she and Howard were seeing one another.

It was hard to keep secrets in a small town. She could already hear Nicky's voice: "What's he like in bed?" But this time she wasn't going to confide in anyone. Not Nicky, or her mother, or Mitch and Joanne.

She put her hand on Howard's arm as a signal that it was time for her to go but he held her back, kissing her one last time and rubbing her breasts with the palm of his hand. Part of her wished he'd suggest that they stay out later. They could drive into the woods and fuck in the backseat. At the same time, she felt sleepy and confused by what was happening and was content with the anticipation of seeing him again in a few days. It was only after she returned to her room, took off her clothes, and stared at herself in the full-length mirror on the door of her closet, that she realized she had left Annette's yellow bag on the floor of the car.

She had planned to catch up on her school work over the weekend at Mitch and Joanne's but ended up sitting on the side of her bed in her room upstairs brushing the knots from her hair and thinking about Howard and Ted. Sometimes she sat with a book open on her knees, only to realize, panic-stricken, that an hour had passed and she hadn't read anything, and sometimes she dropped the pretense that she was even trying to do any work and sat in a chair and stared into space. Her inability to think clearly—"it's as if someone else is controlling my thoughts, not me"—made her understand why some people turned to religion for consolation: it's important to have at least one thing, or person, to depend on in a crisis.

Each thought was a fragment which related in some vague way to the previous thought though often images or faces appeared in her head with no particular connection to what had come before. It was like turning the dial of a radio so that parts of all the songs on all the stations ran together or going to the senior prom with one person and then leaving with someone else and then ending up in bed, as the night progressed, with yet a third person. And when you woke up in the morning someone you had never seen before was lying beside you.

She wanted her parents to think she was no longer upset about Ted.

Each time Mitch or Chris asked her how she felt she said, "Oh, I'm doing great!" or "I feel much better," hoping they wouldn't catch the artificial lilt in her voice.

If anything, they were too concerned about her mental state, too quick to attribute the failure of their marriage as the cause of all her problems. The outbreak of teenage suicides in suburban towns had made parents fearful that the slightest disappointment (not getting into the college "of your choice" or getting cut from the basketball team or breaking up with your lover) might send their child over the edge. And it occurred to Billie, as her mind flitted from one thing to another, as the words on the page of her textbook grew dim, that maybe her parents had a reason to feel worried.

"I want to do well in school," Ted once told her, "but I have no incentive. Wanting something doesn't make it happen."

Billie sat in her room at her father's and stared at the hieroglyphs embedded in the wood above her desk. She drew pictures in red ink in the margin of her notebook: men with pipes and long beards and women in lace brassieres and elaborate corsets. She was sad that her relationship with Ted was over but the fact that it was she who'd made the move to end it gave her a rush of confidence and power, not power over other people but over her own life. The prospects of getting involved with Howard Ryan—"but I'm already involved"—diluted her unhappiness and allowed her to focus on the future as if it were an undiscovered continent, a new moon, something unknown.

At the same time, she worried whether her ability to shift her feelings from one person to another indicated an inability to really feel anything.

"I thought I loved Ted, that was last week, but now I love Howard." She felt like she had known Howard all her life: watching him, those Friday nights, out of the corner of her eye as she sat in the front seat of his Cadillac, driving through the mist in silence. And he'd been watching her too, just waiting for the right moment. The switch from Ted to Howard had taken place too quickly.

Only a week and a half ago she and Ted had made love after school in Ted's mother's house, in the familiar upstairs bedroom with the branches of the old oak scraping the window. He had come on top for a change, the position Billie preferred, though she didn't like being crushed. Sometimes Ted treated her as if she was a life-size blow up doll—the kind advertised in the back of porn magazines. As if she wasn't human. She couldn't imagine making love to an inflated balloon but maybe some people were so frustrated or lonely they would try anything.

It had been one of their best times, really. She was wearing the green skirt with the tangled mass of flowers. It was bunched around her waist. She lifted her legs onto his shoulders and she could feel the tip of his penis against her cervix. "Oh shit," he said, right before he came. She put her hands on his waist as he towered over her before collapsing in her arms.

After they were done, Ted squeezed a new cassette into the tape machine, The Doors singing "Light My Fire." Ted preferred music from another time and place, the music of dead people: Jimi Hendrix, Janis Joplin, Jim Morrison.

Maybe just being this close to another person was all that mattered, Billie thought, yet she never felt totally satisfied.

She could make herself come when she was alone but that was too easy and left her dissatisfied in a different way. With Ted she felt stranded on the brink of the possibility of some pleasure she wanted to perpetuate, the infinite spiral where there were no thoughts, opinions, judgments, no more "I feel this" or "you feel that," a place where all the multiple threads of consciousness vanished into the clear light of day that was the antithesis of this murky haze where it was impossible to even guess what the person lying beside you was feeling.

"It's as if he's not even there, or I'm not."

She thought of the scene in *Madame Bovary*, when shortly after Emma and Charles get married Emma realizes her life isn't turning out as she expected, that her fantasies about "marriage" (which she picked up from reading cheap romances in her convent school) have left her unprepared for the monotony of small town life. To live with a person who doesn't even notice you, who takes you for granted....

Like Emma, most of what Billie knew about people, and about emotions, came from the books she read. She sat at her desk, pen in hand, notebook open, and listened to Mitch and Joanne talking in the room below.

Were they talking about her?

During her week in bed, Mitch had asked her whether she thought she needed some "help"—meaning, she caught on, a therapist, a doctor. The idea of confiding your innermost feelings to someone you didn't know was intriguing, but less so than actually making your own decisions about what to do in your life and then taking the consequences. Taking your own council, so to speak, trusting your instincts. Though therapists didn't normally give advice, they certainly swayed you to do one thing or another. They pointed out directions, they set you on your course.

Without fully realizing it, Billie felt disappointed that her father couldn't help her himself, or come up with a brighter solution. It was as if he didn't have time for her and was shifting the burden onto someone else. Though Mitch always told her she should feel free to talk to him whenever she wanted, he managed to keep his distance, backing away whenever it appeared she had something crucial to tell him. She didn't condemn her parents; compared to Nicky's, or the parents of other people she knew, Mitch and Chris were angels. At least they tried.

Sometimes she stared at the scrap of paper with the phone numbers Whip had given her and remembered how comfortable she had felt talking to him, as if he were her older brother, and even went so far as to call the first number on the list. But when a woman answered she lost her nerve and hung up without saying anything.

Her inability to do her school work and her general feeling of lethargy undercut the potential pleasure of simply relaxing and trying to figure out what her relationship to these men was all about. If she fell too far behind in school she'd be in trouble once the basketball season started; all the interminable practices after school, and then the games, the traveling by bus to small cities like Springfield and Holyoke, and if the team did particularly well all the excitement and pressure of the playoffs.

Every time she tried to concentrate she felt her mind stretching and branching out and then contracting, withdrawing, suddenly splitting into two and then subdividing even further, ameoba-like, until all that remained was a fragment, a shard, a shadow of what had been.

In the past, subjects like the role of the United States in Southeast Asia or the conflict between the Arabs and the Israelis, the famine in Ethiopia, whether the United States had the right to intervene in the governing of another country, should nuclear power plants be demolished, and what about the dumping of nuclear wastes—all these subjects had interested her, she had opinions about everything, but now it was too difficult to think about anything but herself.

She had been assigned to write a ten page research paper on an event that had taken place in the late 1960s (the assassinations of Martin Luther King and Bobby Kennedy, Woodstock, the moon landing, the use of Agent Orange during the Vietnam War, the Manson murders, the Attica uprising, the Marin-county shootout) but it wasn't due for two weeks and Billie was sure that she could do most of the work the night before as long as she gathered all her source material beforehand.

But she still hadn't decided on a topic, nor had she presented the teacher, Ms. Flynn, with an outline. Thinking about the problems of writing the paper was one way of not thinking about herself, a way of narrowing her world to whatever was happening in her immediate surroundings, even if what was happening was next to nothing. This had been Ted's basic philosophy, the only way he could ever accomplish anything, and Billie, as she sat at her cluttered desk listening to the rain slap off the drainpipe, began to wonder if there wasn't at least a modicum of truth contained in Ted's way of thinking.

Nicky called—"I'll come and get you, Hank is here," she shouted into the phone—but Billie made it clear that she had no particular interest in seeing anyone, certainly not Nicky's cousin Hank who would just make a pass at her and pretend to ignore her rebuff and try again. She couldn't just go out and pretend to have fun as if nothing had happened.

"If he's so great," she was tempted to say to Nicky, but didn't, "why don't *you* fuck him?"

It wasn't uncommon for first cousins to become lovers. Large families living in rural settings were notorious for mating among themselves and producing square jawed, blank eyed, offsprings who would in turn mate with other immediate members of their families.

Billie tried to explain as patiently as possible that she didn't want to see anyone, that it wasn't just Hank, and was surprised when Nicky shouted—"What a lousy friend you are!"—and hung up.

Nicky often reminded Billie of Rosemary in *Tender is the Night.* She had the same movie star aura, the same insouciant disregard for other people's feelings. It was too bad Annette and Howard weren't more like Nicole and Dick Diver. The only similarities between Nicole and Annette were that they both liked to drink and were both a little crazy though Billie doubted whether Annette, or anyone else she knew, measured up to Nicole's bouts of insanity.

Neither Nicky nor Ted ever read books unless they had to and there were no books in the Ryan household either, just the usual pile of magazines on the coffee table: *People*, *Sports Illustrated*, *Redbook*, *Vogue*.

Howard subscribed to law journals but barely had time to read them.

"I have the time," he said, "but it's the last thing I ever want to do."

Billie had the impression that Howard was bored with his job, and that if he had the chance he would like to do something else.

"There's still time," she wanted to say, "to become another person."

She was fascinated by the last paragraphs in *Tender*. Nicole and Dick split up; Nicole marries Tommy Barbon and Dick opens a doctor's office, "without success," in Buffalo, New York. From there he moves to Batavia, New York, then to Lockport, Geneva, and finally Hornell. Billie checked the map and learned that all these towns really existed. She couldn't understand what had happened to him, how he'd lost all his ambition, why he never remarried and had another family. Neither Mitch nor Joanne, both English teachers, people who should know, had an adequate clue to the transformation of Dick's psyche.

"He should have gone off with Rosemary," Joanne said, "that was his big chance."

"But Rosemary was just in love with falling in love, she was just using him"—this was Mitch.

"Didn't he ever see his children?" Billie asked.

It was Sunday afternoon, the time of week Billie hated most. Sunday was a day to look forward to if you were part of a family; it was the day the family spent together, ate together, slept late. But if the family was broken into small pieces then maybe you were better off staying in bed most of the day. It was on Sundays that Billie felt an upsurge of anger at her parents for splitting up. When she was with Mitch and Joanne on Sunday she missed Chris; when she spent Sundays with Chris, she longed to be with her father.

If she couldn't be with both of them then she felt like she was nowhere.

She was alone, slipping off the rocks into a gorge, into some infinite reflection, isolate, drifting through space till she reached the bottom.

Some people felt unhappy if they had nothing to do Friday or Saturday nights (often Nicky called her in a panic Saturday afternoon to make plans for that evening since she didn't have a date and couldn't face spending the night alone), but for Billie the worst hour of the week was Sunday, 3 P.M.

She and Mitch had planned a game of one-on-one on the makeshift court behind the house but it was raining and Mitch was in his study correcting papers. Billie sat at her desk upstairs thumbing through an old issue of *Cosmopolitan* which she'd found in a carton in the closet of her room. She turned the pages slowly, staring into the eyes of the models in the ads. The smell of mildew emanated from their golden faces like an exotic perfume. Instinctively, Billie felt that the emphasis on objects and things, on making oneself beautiful, was a false value, yet she couldn't help feeling envious. The women in the magazine formed a composite reflection of someone Billie might want to be, but couldn't.

(If I looked like her, I'd be a model too. The reason she's a model is because she looks a certain way. No matter how much makeup I wear I'll never look like her. In fact, the less makeup I wear the better off I am.)

"The secret to beautiful skin is knowing how to wash your face." "The spontaneity you want and the protection you need." *Ted rolled over and lifted a bottle of beer from the bedside table.*

This was his room, there were pictures of him playing basketball, the pinup of Hendrix with his fiery guitar. As they made love, she let the song on the tape fill her head, like a chant, so that it wasn't necessary to think about anything (her thoughts, when she was with Ted, took the form of a series of complaints: why does he drink so much, why doesn't he touch me).

Sometimes Ted moved quickly, as if he just wanted to get it all over with.

She wanted to take his head between her hands and tell him to slow down.

One minute he was inside her, hovering over her, and the next minute he was gone, lying on top of her like an old log. There was a photo of Ted and his mother, Heather, a frizzy-haired overweight good-natured woman who was genuinely pleased that Billie was interested in her son and who, over dinner, had characterized Ted's previous girlfriends as "a bunch of dogs" while Ted turned red and stared into his plate of baked ham. What I'll miss most are those afternoons in his room, dancing to the music while he lies back, watching.

"At first, two months salary may seem like a lot for a diamond engagement ring...."

Billie turned to an article entitled "Looking for Mr. Goodsex," featuring a photograph of a woman in a red velvet dress stretched out on a narrow sofa while a young blonde man climbed on top of her. The woman's hair matched her dress and fell in a luxurious wave over the edge of the couch. Her eyes were closed. According to the article, sex was best when the lovers were already friends, when they trusted one another and felt genuine concern for each other's pleasure. Multiple orgasms aren't important. Quality, the quality of one orgasm, is more important than number. In fact it isn't necessary to fuck ("have intercourse") to express your feelings. Not always, anyway; sometimes affection is enough. A man is not a sex machine and must be stimulated, especially an older man, who might require direct stimulation. Most women are indifferent to the size of a man's penis.

Most women are indifferent....

Billie closed the magazine and thought of the conversations in school among the girls on the basketball team about the size of the penises of the men they slept with. The only reason people made love to one another, or so Billie sometimes thought, was so they could talk about it afterwards with their friends. Or with anyone. Ted's penis had always seemed huge to her, but then she didn't have many others to compare it with.

Downstairs, Joanne played Satie's "Trois Gynopedies" on the baby grand in the living room. It was soothing, like the October rain, but it was the kind of calm that usually preceded some manic outburst: who could predict the new trajectory? How far could the mind leap?

Billie knew that Joanne would be all too willing to talk with her if she wanted, and often talking with Joanne was more satisfying than talking to Mitch or Chris, but Billie, for once in her life, was at a loss about where to begin. She felt embarrassed about telling anyone the reasons why she and Ted broke up. To describe him as a budding alcoholic didn't seem fair and she had no inclination to discuss her feelings about Howard (it was hard enough to even articulate them to herself). She imagined herself creating a hypothetical "friend" who had become involved with a married man, just to see what Joanne would say. But it was hard to fool anyone, especially someone who knew you, and Billie doubted she could tell the story without giving herself away.

She helped Joanne prepare dinner —baked flounder ("watch out for the bones"), cauliflower and corn bread—and afterward played chess with Mitch. Joanne built a fire and sat in the rocking chair reading Poe. Sipping cognac. It was cold for the beginning of October.

"Are you going to play basketball this year?"

It was time to start practicing; all this sitting around, brooding, wasn't good for her. She should be running five miles a day; more than that, though she was confident (the same way she was confident about her schoolwork) that she could get into shape quickly, a few weeks before the season began.

"Should...should...should...."

Billie hated the word. A log rolled over and some sparks scattered onto the stones. She wondered what Ted was doing and how long it would take him to find a new girlfriend. If he didn't go to college, and the prospects were dim unless he received a basketball scholarship, he'd end up working in the garage or in one of the malls or maybe, as a last resort, he'd take a job as stock boy at Caldwell's, the supermarket on Main Street which Nicky's parents owned. The thought of Ted and Nicky working together in such close proximity made Billie laugh.

The Farmer's Almanac had predicted one of the worst winters in years. Joanne wore a long red peasant's dress with a fake bib and black tights. She'd had one important relationship before marrying Mitch, a man twice her age with whom she'd lived for two years.

"He wanted to have kids and I didn't," was her excuse for why they split up.

Billie noticed that Joanne was quieter, more meditative than usual, and that she and Mitch had barely exchanged two words with one another all weekend. Billie was tempted to ask her if anything was wrong. Did she have a migraine? Was she getting her period?

The problem of being caught up in your own dilemmas is that you forget that other people have problems too. And so no one ever makes any attempt to help anyone else and if you want to talk to someone about your problems you have to hire a stranger at eighty dollars an hour (if you're lucky), someone who will listen and instruct and point out patterns of behavior, someone to assuage your fears and assure you that nothing you do is your fault, a person who will actually take on the guise of your mother or father or lover, anyone you want them to be, until you understand beyond a doubt why you're incapable of loving anyone, or why you want to please everyone even if they hate you.

It was still raining Monday when Mitch drove her to school. A single player was dribbling a ball between the puddles on the newly paved asphalt court and for a moment, from the back, Billie thought it was Ted. It wasn't, but the image reminded her that she might meet him by chance during the course of the day. She hadn't seen or heard from him since he strolled out of the Ryan's kitchen more than a week before, and she wanted to be prepared just in case he ignored her.

"How are you?"

She said the words to herself in the same way she would say them to Ted, with emphasis on the "are," then with emphasis on the "you," not certain which sounded better, frightened he'd catch a trace of insincerity in her voice. And what would Ted, who rarely spoke anyway (for all she knew, he might pretend he didn't see her), answer in return?

She wanted to ask Mitch if anything was wrong with Joanne but it occurred to her that what was wrong with Joanne might have to do with Mitch, that something was going wrong between them. And then she wondered, if this was true, whether she really wanted to know. The last thing she wanted to hear was that some other segment of her family was falling apart.

Hopefully, whatever was troubling them would pass.

Maybe Joanne's mood reflected an expression of solidarity with Billie because of her problems with Ted, "I understand how you must feel," meaning that all men are alike, something Billie didn't believe was true.

Arnie and Richard were different from Ted but maybe, in the long run, they were more alike than different, and maybe people were right when they advised you to get to know a wide variety of people and in that way improve the chance of meeting someone who was noticeably different from all the others, someone who's your "type" and whom you might contemplate living with for thirty or forty years. If Arnie and Richard had shown some interest in her who knows what might have happened.

If Mitch and Joanne split up does that mean I'll never see Joanne again?

It depends. This is my mother, this is my father—and everyone else (except my own lovers) are transitory characters who could drop out of my life at any given moment and vanish forever.

The high school was a low, sprawling red brick structure, surrounded by playing fields and a parking lot, with a water tower and a trio of smokestacks at one end that made it look like a factory. Sports was a big deal at East Winston, not only to the students but to their parents, many of whom had graduated from the same school years before. It was easier to raise money for a new football field or a new gym than for laboratory equipment or new books for the library. Whenever one of the teams won the state championship, they celebrated with a midnight parade through town, a fire truck leading the way. Everyone drunk, waving pennants, hanging onto the side of the truck for dear life.

She started for her locker, which was in the basement, careful not to make eye contact with the students passing her in the hall. The idea that she might be the object of anyone's attention (did everyone in the school know about her and Ted? were they whispering about her behind her back?) gave her a secret rush of pleasure, yet it embarrassed her as well, much the same way she felt when she won an award for her essays or when she scored an important basket. Billie knew that people envied her for the ease with which she managed to juggle life as a student and a basketball star and that envy, taken to an extreme, was a form of hatred.

She had even encountered such feelings from Nicky who was supposedly her best friend.

She thought she saw Ted's head veering towards her from the end of the hall but once again it turned out to be someone else. She wanted to see him, get the initial confrontation over with. Maybe some day we can even be friends.

Before going to class, she stopped off at Coach Miller's office and picked up a copy of the basketball schedule. There were no Friday night games until early December which meant she could continue babysitting for the Ryans. From behind the doors of the gym she heard the thud of sneakers against wood as the first gym class of the morning ran laps around the perimeter. It was a hollow sound, like the beating of a human heart. She paused outside the display cabinet and stared at her reflection. There were the trophies, like Greek statuary, commemorating the heroics of the past.

There was Ted, in a photograph of the previous year's team, number 10, in gold and red, refusing to smile, surrounded by his teammates who were obviously overjoyed at something Ted was missing. What was it? Why was he so contrary about everything?

Billie opened her locker and dumped the contents of her shoulder bag onto the shelf. All she needed was a notebook, her social studies textbook and a copy of *Tender is the Night*. Monday was her easiest day: social studies, study hall, English—that was the morning. Trigonometry and Spanish in the afternoon. No basketball practice.

A whistle blew, it was Coach Miller, no doubt, in the center of the gym, and for a moment Billie wished she was in there, behind the heavy wooden doors, breathing hard, her blood circulating freely, the ceiling lights reflecting the tiny bubbles of sweat on her eyelids. Wasn't it better to be this physical creature than a person with a mind that was cut off from the rest of her body? It had been awhile since she'd pushed herself to the edge of exhaustion—then beyond, to the point where pain and pleasure intertwined. It was the same feeling she wanted to reach when she made love but it never happened.

"Don't come so quickly," she hissed in Ted's ear, but by the time she said it he was gone.

She entered the classroom a few minutes late. Ms. Flynn, the social studies teacher, was writing a series of dates on one side of the blackboard: next to each date was a number, the price of a gallon of oil for each particular year.

"Today we're going to discuss...."

In just a few months, Ms. Flynn had become one of the school's most popular teachers. Most of her colleagues had chosen the profession of teaching as a a last resort and it was rare for the school to find someone fresh from college who was truly devoted to her work. Part of the pleasure of coming to class was simply to stare at Ms. Flynn ("you can call me Elaine") and take mental notes about what she was wearing from day to day.

It wasn't difficult to shape the contour of her body under her clothing and imagine what it might feel like lying with her naked on a bed. The clothing she wore seemed to be inviting you to touch her body.

This morning she was wearing a purple wraparound skirt, white fishnet stockings, and a long cream-colored shirt with a checkered pattern and wide collars. And didn't she wear the same shirt last week? Did she ever wear the same clothing twice? Most of the students had never seen anyone quite like her before: it was as if a model had stepped out of the pages of *Vogue* into all of their lives.

"Today we're going to discuss how the price of oil...."

All the guys in the class had a crush on Ms. Flynn—there was a heated debate among them whether she wore any underwear at all—but treated her less like a potential lover than an older sister: if anyone tried to disrupt the class they'd be shouted down immediately.

There were always rumors about Ms. Flynn's lovelife, whether she had any boyfriends. Someone claimed she had seen her holding hands with Mr. Masters, the biology teacher. Another had seen her on line at Caldwell's supermarket with Mr. Dawson, the recently divorced assistant principal.

Someone else said that she'd been married before but that her husband had died in a traffic accident.

She sat on the edge of her desk and crossed her legs, shifting a small piece of chalk from one hand to the other. She could read the local telephone directory, if she wanted, and everyone would dutifully copy down the numbers. Unlike most of the teachers in the school, she knew everyone's name by heart. Often when she called on one of the guys her question was greeted with a dazed expression, as if her voice was interrupting a fantasy: they were alone in the classroom, it was late afternoon, and as she bent forward over the desk he lifted her skirt from behind....

Everyone stared at the piece of chalk, at her red open toed sandals, at her necklace of amethyst stones.

"You should meet the new Social Studies teacher," Billie had once told Ted, raising her eyebrows; if anything, he would be intrigued by the way she dressed.

A wisp of red hair fell across one side of her face, like Veronica Lake, and she brushed it aside, a gesture she would repeat fifty times in the course of a day.

Nicky sat up front, wide-eyed, pen in hand. In most of her classes she had trouble staying awake, but Ms. Flynn's 8:30 class was like an extension of her dreams. It made her think that she too could become a teacher some day. When she listened to Ms. Flynn she realized that she could do anything, that the world held more potential than working forty hours a week at her parents' store.

Greg Sorrells sat directly in front of Billie. He was stocky, a football player, and had been one of Nicky's first lovers when they were both sophomores. He wore his hair very short and his shirt open to the waist, even on the coldest days. She stared at the black thorn-like stubble sticking up from the skin on the back of his neck and tried to imagine Nicky and he in bed. She imagined Greg's penis disappearing into Nicky's mouth.

Across the aisle, Jamie Mikowlowski was busily writing in her notebook. When she finished she ripped the page from her book, folded it, and passed the note across the aisle to Marta Meade. Marta read the note, smiled, and began composing one of her own. There were rumors that Jamie and Marta were lovers but no one knew for sure. Marta was from Norway but had lived in France as a child. Her parents were separated and Marta lived with her mother and grandmother. Her father was remarried. She was tall, blonde and spectacularly thin, with islands of freckles covering her shoulders and arms, and Billie loved watching her during swimming, the way she seemed to hold her body suspended in mid-air as she dived off the board into the pool, her gold hair trailing behind.

Ted once told Billie that Greg Sorrells was spreading rumors that Nicky was frigid, but Billie never confronted her friend with this news.

Maybe, if you're frigid, it has something to do with the way your so-called lover is treating you. People tend to blame themselves for everything without ever realizing that someone else might be equally at fault.

Ms. Flynn walked to the blackboard and wrote the letters O P E C.

When she turned her back to the class, all the students looked up from their notebooks and stared intently at the curve of her ass, and then at the gold bracelet around her ankle.

Billie, who sat in the back of the room, took out her pen, opened her notebook, and wrote the name "Howard," encircling it with a heart. Her plan was to cut school during the afternoon and meet Howard in the parking lot behind the library. From there they'd drive to a motel—"I know the owner, don't worry, no one will find out, you'll be home by five"—where he'd rented a room for the day.

She stared at the back of Nicky's head and wished her friend would turn around and make some kind of gesture to show she was no longer angry.

They'd had fights before but Billie's unwillingness to see Hank was a sore point in their relationship. Billie remembered days when she wished she looked like Nicky; it was hard to be friends with someone who was so confident about her ability to attract men. Whenever they were together and met a man for the first time, he would invariably direct his attention to Nicky, and ignore her. Yet Billie didn't doubt her own attractiveness: it wasn't as obvious as Nicky's, but more accessible. Ted once said that most of the guys at school thought Nicky unapproachable, echoing Nicky's own fear that potential boyfriends were scared off by her looks.

At the end of the class all the girls formed a circle around Ms. Flynn's desk, while the guys loitered at the door of the classroom, like hanger-ons at a party, hoping the teacher had some special chore for them to perform.

Nicky, wearing a short leather skirt, a black turtleneck and black patterned stockings, sat at her desk making faces at herself in a small oval mirror.

"Are you still angry?" Billie asked.

"I'm hurt. And I'm angry too. You don't understand how you can do something that might hurt me." Nicky looked up and realized that the other students, as well as Ms. Flynn, had stopped what they were doing and were staring at them. She stuffed her makeup into her pocketbook, closed her spiral notebook, and followed Billie out of the room.

"I try to understand you, but it doesn't seem fair. Whenever you have a problem you call me up and ask for my help, but when I call you—"

"But you didn't have a problem. You know I don't like Hank and you know that—"

"It's just a date. A simple date. I wasn't asking you to marry him. You might have just gone out with us or come by the house when he was here."

"If I thought he wanted to be friends with me I'd have no trouble but you know what happens whenever I see him. And the last thing I want these days is some asshole coming on to me."

"Listen, you don't have to worry about it, he's gone, the asshole is gone, he went back to California. He only stayed a few days."

"You mean he went back to California because I wouldn't see him? I don't believe it."

"Don't give yourself so much credit. He was bored here."

"I don't run an escort service," Billie said. "I can't believe you're so angry. It's no big deal."

"What I want is no big deal, that's what you say, but when you have a problem," she had to control herself, "the world stops breathing."

They were standing in the center of the hallway and anyone who wanted to pass had to circle around them. Occasionally, someone said "Hi Nicky" or "Good to see you, Billie" and in turn each of them looked up and nodded or smiled without missing a beat in their own conversation. In Billie's eyes, Nicky had taken the form of an ogre, intent on torturing her for something she hadn't done, and for a moment she was tempted to admit that everything Nicky said was true, if only this person—she was no longer "Nicky" but "this person"—would stop hating her.

"It's not Hank, it's everything. You don't pay enough attention to me, you never do what I want. This is just the tip of the iceberg. I've been feeling this way for years. It's what I said on the phone: you're a lousy friend. You don't care about anyone but yourself."

"You're wrong, I care about everyone, I care too much, that's my problem," Billie protested, and burst into tears.

He'd been married to Annette for eight years and I was his first lover, at least that's what he said. His first girlfriend. It was all new to him.

He and Annette slept in separate beds. "We stopped making love," he told me, "after the girls were born." I felt sorry for him and wanted to please him. It was my inclination, the desire to give pleasure, to make someone happy. But it was different with Howard, at least at first, because he never took me for granted. Every time he touched me it was like I was giving him permission to do something he never imagined would ever happen, not in his wildest dreams. He'd become resigned to a life of suffering (though by this point it wasn't even suffering, nothing that strong, just an acceptance of fate: this is the way life had turned out to be). He'd forgotten what it was like to desire and be desired, much in the same way I'd forgotten what it was like to be touched during the months that I was with Ted. (Maybe "forgotten" isn't the right word: it was something I'd never experienced.) I loved Ted, I accepted his way of being, but it wasn't enough. "Acceptance" is how I defined love. I wanted to like what he liked, as if I had no "self" of my own. The idea of feeling selfless dominated my feelings of love. "Lift up your skirt," Ted said, and I did.

—We're in the shower at the motel, his fingers inside me as we rock back and forth under the spray. It's too hot at first then the water turns lukewarm then hot again then suddenly it's too cold and I scream out half in shock at the change of temperature and the rush of pleasure as he moves his fingers. I'm taking a shower at the motel. "Can I join you?" he asks, as he parts the curtain.

This was a different time and I wondered if we could fuck this way, standing up, facing one another. Howard's an inch taller than I am and I don't understand why it doesn't work (I have my soapy hand on his cock and I'm trying to put it in but it's impossible, it keeps slipping out and we're both laughing). His skin is white, blonde, bleached out, colorless.

The hair on his chest is turning gray. Another time I'm in the shower alone and he's waiting in bed. I stand at the door of the bedroom, in the steam, my wet shoulders, my hair piled up on top of my head. He's lying on his side watching me in the afternoon light through the hazy yellow curtains and for a moment I remember the afternoons in Ted's room in that same half-light when I used to dress up and dance for him. The thought excites me.... Should I tell Howard about Ted?

—After we make love I put my arms around him, his lips pressed against the side of my neck, and let him sleep for fifteen minutes. It takes all my strength not to fall asleep as well but I remain vigilant about it all as if making sure we both get home at the right time is my new job. My new vocation. If we want to see each other we have to be careful.

Every Monday I leave school early and meet him in the parking lot behind the library. We drive to the motel, I want to stop the car and make love in the rain on the side of the road, in the front seat of the Cadillac, in the heat from the vents with the windshield wipers attacking the drops on the glass like a deadly scythe. "We'll be there in a minute," he says, more patient than I. I've been thinking about making love to him all week.

When I sit upstairs in my room and try to study I see his face, his hands, the curve of his shoulders. The wrinkles in his forehead.

The owner of the motel is the brother of one of Howard's clients and they have an "arrangement" so we never have to check in when we arrive but it's hard to imagine that no one's peeking through a curtain as we emerge from the car and run through the rain to our room. Howard has his own key and there are never any other cars parked outside the other units. The name of the motel is the Acorn Acres (it was the fruit of the trees, our sustenance), on the outskirts of Carmel, about fifteen miles from the center of East Winston. We meet every Monday in the parking lot outside the library.

Out of habit, I wear skirts and dresses whenever I'm with Howard, but unlike Ted he never comments about my clothing.

—Even after we become lovers I continue to babysit for the Ryans.

I arrive at seven Friday evening, just like always, and sit in the kitchen with Sara and Emma while Howard stalks through the rooms like an expectant father and Annette preens in front of her mirror upstairs. Ever since the night that I broke up with Ted she's been overly friendly towards me but I don't know if she knows about Howard and I or why her mood changed so dramatically. In a way, I prefer the old hostile Annette.

When they get home she doesn't stumble upstairs or pass out on the rug like in the old days, but joins me in the living room to discuss her night out. Her monologue takes the form of a series of complaints about the dreariness of small town life. I pretend that I'm interested in everything she says, but all the time I'm counting to myself, the numbers are like a song, watching Howard's shadow as he stands at the door of the room, like a security guard, listening, waiting. I'm counting the seconds until it's time to go. It's getting cold but I'm wearing a skirt (not Ted's skirt, I won't wear that one now) so Howard can touch me in the car. We sit in the front seat of the Cadillac under the trees across from my mother's house and kiss for a long time with his fingers moving inside me. If I screamed no one would hear. If I cried out from pleasure no one would mind.

—It all started that September, the night I broke up with Ted. Easy to say the words—"I don't think we should see each other any more"—yet hard to be sure that I was doing the right thing. I could see the pulse in Ted's neck as he swallowed under the strain of hearing my words, as if the meaning was something tangible which he could digest and absorb, a kind of ineffable music which pierced the air waves at a pitch only an animal could hear, too high for human ears.

What's right or wrong for you isn't necessarily what's right or wrong for everyone and most people spend their lives in the vortex of a storm of doubt about whether they're acting selfishly or in everyone else's best interests. Yet at some point you have to say "this is what I want." At eighteen, who can be sure? I want Ted, I want Howard, I want my parents to live together again. Does Ted want me? I want to be alone, long evenings in my room, listening to the rain.

Even now, so many years later, I like to read in bed for at least an hour every morning with a cup of coffee. (My lover makes the coffee and joins me in bed.) It's what I think of as some kind of ultimate small pleasure, like fresh flowers, like lying on the grass in a clearing staring up through the mangled branches of a tree.

There's the sun behind the leaves and the clouds moving across the sky. I like the sound of water nearby. Mostly, I want to be wanted. My instinct, my second skin, tells me that Ted's love isn't enough. He never touches me when we make love, he doesn't care about what I feel. He never tells me what he's feeling. I ask him to leave, I have to, no matter how painful.

He's gone and I'm in the kitchen at Howard and Annette's scraping the food off the dinner dishes to pass the time.

It's Friday night. I'm wearing my long red tight skirt with a zipper up the back, black leotards and a white blouse with Chinese letters.

—One day I came home early and saw my father's car parked outside. It was mid-December and I'd twisted my knee during basketball practice. Dr. Bowa, the team trainer, wrapped my knee in an ace bandage and told me to soak it in a hot bath. I wanted to go into the house and lie down but I didn't want to surprise my parents. What were they doing together? Why wasn't my mother at work? The house looked dark from the outside and I felt like I might be intruding on something that didn't have anything to do with me or was beyond my understanding even though the people involved were my parents and this was my house.

When I was a child I'd get into bed with my parents on weekend mornings, maneuver between them so that I was touching both of them at the same time. I didn't want to separate them but to join them: possibly even then I sensed that everything was falling apart.

And then I remember other nights, lying in bed, listening to their voices. They were talking too loud, not laughing, but the level went beyond high spiritedness, as if one were drunk and the other angry and the combination of the two created a maniacal cacophony which continued till it reached a feverish edge, subsiding in the same maniacal fashion as the sudden descent of a roller coaster or waterfall.

I saw my father's car, a blue Toyota, parked in front of the house. I stared at it for a long time, not knowing whether its presence was a sign of good or bad news. It was definitely a portent of something but I didn't know what that could be. (I'd never returned home from school and found his car parked in front of my mother's house before and he rarely ever visited, except when I was sick. But then again, how often had I returned home early from school? Possibly Mitch and Chris met and made love once a week, much in the same way Howard and I met every Monday in the parking lot behind the library and drove off, secretly, to the Acorn Acres?)

I hobbled to the end of the block, not wanting to interrupt whatever my parents were doing, and sat on a bench near a bus stop and waited. It was cold, and whenever a bus pulled up the passengers looked down at me through the tinted windows, people who knew who I was but who didn't recognize me since for a moment I had become a ward of the state, an orphan in the storm, a transient on her way out of town, a runaway baby hitch-hiker: why would anyone sit on a bench in the cold if they had some place to go?

All my life I've had fantasies of waiting in cramped, isolated spaces, the crag of a mountaintop buffeted by 80 mile per hour winds or a cave on a beach in the eye of a hurricane, summoning up the strength to survive until help arrived. I'd sit in Howard's car, Monday afternoons, waiting for him to appear at the back door of the library. And as he approached the car I would think to myself, in wonder: "This is not the man of my dreams."

—I bruise easily, and Howard always leaves marks on my arms. If anyone asks me about them I'll say I fell during practice.

—I can't call Howard at night (he calls me when Annette isn't home) but we manage to talk at least once every day. Sometimes I call him at his office above the library from the pay phone at school or when I get home.

"I dreamed about you last night," I tell him. All I want to do, when I'm not with him, is soak in a hot bath up to my chin. I bring a stack of novels to the bathroom with me but most of the time I just lie back with my eyes closed, enveloped in a cloud of steam.

My mother stands at the bathroom door and gives me a worried look. She's still concerned about the way I've been acting since Ted and I split up and the fact that I can't confide in her about Howard creates a small bridge between us, as if I'm on one side with my secrets and she's on the other side with hers.

Monday afternoons at the motel and late Friday nights when Howard drives me home are the only times we're really together. We talk about what it might be like to spend a night in each other's arms, to wake up in the morning in the same bed, something I've never done with anyone.

We talk about what would happen if he decided to leave Annette.

—I read my favorite poem, "What lips my lips have kissed," by Edna St. Vincent Millay, and weep. It's Christmas, I hate the vacations, anything that interrupts my routine with Howard. He's going to spend the day with Annette and the kids.

Chris prepares a big mid-afternoon dinner for all her single friends and their kids (no husbands to flirt with, alas). I spend the day cooking (roast beef, baked potatoes stuffed with green peppers, peas and carrots, pecan pie) and go over to Mitch and Joanne's in the evening. For them, it's like any other evening, they don't do anything special. Mitch gives me a two-volume boxed edition of the collected writings of Henry David Thoreau. (Earlier, Chris had given me a Vidal Sassoon hair dryer.)

Joanne gives me a skirt—"another skirt!" I remind her—with a colorful animal print: elephants, tigers, giraffes, zebras. I wonder what Ted would think, I wish he was there to comment, his chin resting in the palm of his hand, while I twirled around.

It's easy to forget what went wrong and just remember the good parts of our relationship and sometimes I regret ever breaking up with him.

We sit around the fire and I sip from a glass of cognac, just to pass the time. I'm passing the time until I can see Howard again.

We're in the motel and he gives me my present. It's a necklace of gemstones: citrine, blue topaz, pink and green tormaline, amethyst and aquamarine. The stones feel cool against my bare skin. I'm tempted to ask him what he bought for Annette, but I don't.

The colors of the stones reflect the light pouring through the pleats in the venetian blinds. I lie on my stomach, head in pillow, legs apart, and wait for Howard to get out of the shower. (Ted would love my new skirt.)

—Eduardo Narcimento, the Mexican exchange student and the star of the track team, asks me for a date. He's one of the best dressed guys at school, very proper and formal, and I amaze myself by not saying "no" when he asks. I give him my phone number. Possibly if I begin going on dates with someone, Chris and Mitch will stop acting so concerned about me.

I tell Chris that I'm going out with Eduardo Narcimento and she beams. Apparently, he comes from a wealthy family in Mexico City. He's a star athlete and does well in school, just like me. He speaks perfect English. His main interest is biology—at least that's what I learn from our brief conversations in the hallway at school. Unlike Ted, who didn't even come into the house on our first date, Eduardo is a model of decorum and sits in the living room with Chris while I get ready. When I enter the living room he stands up. He's wearing a dark blue blazer and a matching tie against a white shirt with wide collars, tapered slacks, black loafers. I've never gone out with anyone who wears a tie. I'm wearing my new skirt, the one Joanne bought me for Christmas.

Eduardo talks about his family, most of whom live in Brazil, and especially about his sister with whom he lived after his parents died. Now he lives in the house of the track coach, Manny Assuado. Meester Assuado, as Eduardo calls him. He hopes to get a track scholarship to an Ivy League college but he isn't sure which one or whether he's good enough. I wonder what he would do if I took his hand in the movie theater and placed it under my skirt. He looks so rigid, in his new jacket, so straight-laced, so horribly correct.

He doesn't drink or smoke and I'm his first date "in America," or so he says. "But didn't you have any girlfriends in South America?" He nods his head, meaning "yes," but that doesn't mean he isn't a virgin. (He might have lost his virginity with a prostitute for all I know.)

It would be wonderful to sleep with him once, to show him how easy it all is, but then what? I'm filled with a feeling of power that involves initiating action rather than just following someone else's lead.

We park outside Chris's house and I ask him if he'd like to come in for a beer. Or maybe a cup of tea? Chris's bedroom is dark but that doesn't mean she's asleep. "I'm having trouble sleeping," she told me recently, and I wonder if her new problems have anything to do with my father.

Christmas holiday is over and Howard and I continue to meet: every Monday afternoon we drive to the Acorn Acres. What kind of tea do they drink in Mexico City? In Brazil? The flame beneath the pot on the stove is blue, the water is boiling. As I cross the room I can tell Eduardo's staring at me, watching the faces of the animals on my skirt.

—Every Monday afternoon it becomes more difficult to separate. How much time do we have? Two hours, sometimes three. Annette spends two mornings a week with her lover Bob; she calls Howard every afternoon and if he isn't in his office she gets suspicious.

"If she knew we were sleeping together she'd kill me—and you too." Yet doesn't it bother him that Annette fucks other men?

It's getting dark as we leave the motel and there are one or two cars parked in the slots outside the other rooms, a crust of dirty snow around the rim of the swimming pool, and a light on in the office where through parted curtains I can see a woman with red hair smoking a cigarette and talking on the phone, a black and white television bathing the room in anonymity. (I can glimpse that fragment of a scene in the corner of my memory as if it was yesterday.)

It's almost time to leave and I'm standing in the bathroom of the motel, fully dressed, studying myself in the mirror, when Howard comes up behind me, lifts my skirt and begins rubbing my clitoris with his index finger. "I thought we had to leave." I lean back against him and close my eyes.

—Annette's uncle is dying. "She's flying back to Indianapolis for a week," Howard says.

He asks me to come over and help out with the kids. I sit on the familiar bed upstairs, reading books to Emma and Sara. My mother will come and pick me up at nine. Howard tells me that Annette used to be the Hog Queen of Indiana. He shows me photographs. (We have to be careful not to be overly affectionate around the kids.)

It's hard to imagine her in a bathing suit, with a crown on her head, a red banner with the words "Hog Queen" rippling in the wind behind her, but there she is, on a stage next to a giant red-faced man in a Stetson with his stomach bulging out of the lower buttons of his monogrammed shirt. "That's Annette's old man," Howard says.

I love Emma and Sara and wonder what it would be like to live with them. Howard keeps hinting that he's going to leave Annette. "And be with you," he always tacks on.

We lie down on the living room floor where Ted and I used to make love. "I have some money, we can go to New York together...or Boston...you can go to school." I listen as he tells me the possible scenarios of life after Annette, but I don't say anything.

I go there every night. I help with dinner and put the kids to bed. Annette calls, her uncle is dead, she's going to stay a few extra days. The door of the bedroom is unlocked and I go inside and stand in front of the wall-length closet with sliding doors and stare at the dresses and skirts and suits and blouses, some of them still with price tags, all with designer labels, and the dozens of boxes of shoes, the bureau drawers overflowing with nightgowns and bras and slips. "I don't sleep in this room any more," Howard says.

I sit on top of him on the living room floor and lift my skirt just the way I used to do with Ted. His penis isn't as large as Ted's but it seems to go deeper inside me. I close my eyes and pretend I'm making love to Ted.

—My parents separated when I was thirteen. I'd lie in bed listening to them talking at the kitchen table, their voices subdued, not angry. The days of fighting were over by now and they were resigned to the fact that living together was impossible, that "trying to work things out" (how long had they been trying?) was no longer a solution.

"There's a house across town," I heard my father say. I knew that there was another person involved, my father's girlfriend, and that perhaps some day soon, if not immediately, I would acquire a new relation, a "stepmother," that my parents were creating a situation where I'd be forced to choose between them, almost on a daily basis, that in many cases they'd make the decision for me ("tonight you're going to stay at your father's") whether I liked the plan or not, that I'd never have both of them again on my terms which were in fact the simplest terms of all: that they stick to the agreement they made when they decided to have a child.

I know that people with children get divorced every day and that numbers are comforting but that doesn't make each individual situation less free of misery or anger.

It's hard to imagine, with all that turmoil in the world, why the surface of the earth just doesn't boil over, like some Biblical scene where God, in his patriarchal fervor, throws up his hands in frustration and decides to wipe out the entire population of the world and start again. My parents had loved one another enough to have a child; then they'd stopped loving one another, but here I was, the product of that initial feeling, not a commodity that could be hauled downstairs and placed in a trunk in the basement after it had outlived its usefulness, but real live breathing flesh and blood, as real as they both were, a person with a heart and a mind of her own.

There's a chance that if I didn't exist they would have separated long before they did and I can't fault them for wanting to find their own version of happiness and peace of mind and I can't say that they made their decision not to live together without thinking about me and I know it's too selfish of me to wish they'd stay together because of me, for me, faking their love so that I didn't think all people who lived together hated each other. I knew there was something askew between my parents but I never knew whether it was a temporary or permanent situation, whether one day my father would return from work and my mother would greet him at the door as if she were happy to see him, fling her arms around him with true feeling instead of not even acknowledging his presence when he came in. It was that lack of acknowledgement that I witnessed time and time again, as if she truly didn't care whether he returned or not.

Yet I knew she did care and while she pretended to occupy herself with other things I knew she was really waiting for him and that I was waiting too. I didn't know why my father was late (why was he creating problems by not coming home on time?) or whether it was my mother, something she had done, that was keeping him away. There was no way I could ignore the tension in the air when they were together, and most often when my father did finally return I took it as a cue to go upstairs to my room and close the door. Maybe they needed their privacy, I reasoned. Maybe I was getting in the way with all my questions?

Often, when I was at a friend's house, I heard another set of parents fighting, and I began to think that maybe this feeling of hostility was a kind of status quo (less the exception than the rule) among people who were married. "My parents fight all the time," Nicky said, after I told her that Mitch was leaving. "Maybe they'll split up too."

One afternoon I returned from school and my father was no longer there. All the books and papers in his study were gone. The closet was empty; the hangers banged together as I slammed the door. My mother had warned me that she and my father were thinking of living separately but neither had said "when" this monumental event was going to take place.

Possibly they thought, since he was only moving across town, they could act casual about the change. I could see them both every day or talk to them on the phone. I was still going to school, I had the same friends as I had yesterday, my parents were still my parents even if they didn't live under the same roof.

Yet I felt hurt that they didn't sit down and discuss this new arrangement with me even if they were presenting their decision as a *fait accompli*. Wasn't it my business too?

—Howard doesn't want me to go out with Eduardo Narcimento. He doesn't trust me when I tell him that I'm simply using Eduardo as a kind of cover so my parents and everyone else will stop wondering if I'm going to have a nervous breakdown. If I tell my parents that I'm going out with someone new they'll stop watching me so closely.

"Do you let him touch your breasts?"

Howard reaches out and cups my breasts with his palm, more like a slave market auctioneer than my lover, as a way of stating my body is his property and that no one else can go near.

His attitude towards me begins to change as soon as I start seeing Eduardo and no doubt Howard can tell that I'm not being completely honest with him even though it's true that Eduardo never touches me and that I can barely get him to kiss me good night. I'm not merely using Eduardo as a cover but I'm truly enjoying our time together.

(It's a relief not to have to lie to everyone about what I'm doing and when Chris asks me if I'm going out I can say "Eduardo's picking me up at 8.")

I meet Howard in his car behind the library and we drive, like always, to the motel. He doesn't say a word. Every gesture sends off flares of anger and contempt. Instead of giving me his cigarette to light while he drives he jams the car lighter with his thumb and turns the radio full blast.

"Why are you angry?"

But I know, he doesn't have to say anything.

"I'll stop seeing him if you want" is all I can think of saying. I want to tell Howard to stop being an idiot, to trust me, while another part of me is flattered that he's so jealous.

The truth is that he has reason to feel jealous, and that it's just a matter of time, I know it is, before Eduardo and I make love.

—Sometimes I burst into tears when I'm with Howard. He doesn't understand. I go past a point where even I don't know what I'm doing or why I'm doing it or where I am and when I come back to being this person in this bed in this room I get sad and burst into tears.

And then a voice says "turn over" and I do. I lie on my stomach and let him do whatever he wants.

—Howard doesn't like *Madame Bovary*. He read a hundred pages and then stopped, so I gave him a copy of *The Sun Also Rises* instead. "I think I read this in college," he says, with no real interest. He lost the habit of reading after getting out of law school and doesn't even bother with trash novels by writers like Robert Ludham or Richard Condon which some of his colleagues read to escape the so-called pressures of the real world. In college he read summary outlines of the books that were assigned to him.

"You mean you read every word?" he said when I tried to explain that the descriptive parts of a book were as important as the dialogue. I think he'd understand me better if he read more.

At least it would give us something to talk about.

—"I don't understand Howard Ryan."

I write this in my journal. It's the end of March. The end of the basketball season.

I don't understand, this is what I really mean, why I ever thought I might be in love with him. It's hard to imagine being in love and then not being in love without understanding how that happens or how often it can happen in the course of one lifetime.

Eduardo is the perfect gentleman and seems content with a simple good night kiss but Howard is furious that I'm going out with him and assumes that I'm fucking him too.

"I don't know why I love you," I want to say. There's a feeling of tension in the air between us now that wasn't there before and this feeling dominates all the time we're together, even when we're in bed in the motel. I try to steer the conversation around to books. We discuss the character of Meursault, in *The Stranger*, one of the few books I gave him which he actually reads.

"I would have killed the Arab too," he says. He doesn't like *Madame Bovary* and I wonder if it's because the relationship between Emma and Charles reminds him too much of his relationship with Annette.

"Howard is like Charles," I write in my journal, but I realize there's a big difference between them. Charles never questions Emma's fidelity (he's blind to the fact that she might be sleeping with other men) while Howard is fully aware that Annette sleeps with as many men as possible. He seems more interested in *The Sun Also Rises* but can't understand why Jake Barnes couldn't sleep with women. What's the nature of this war injury? (Sometimes I find it hard to believe we're talking about the same book.)

It's tense in the car as we drive from the parking lot behind the library to our room at the Acorn Acres. The only time Howard ever laughs is when we're in bed. I no longer ask him when he's going to leave Annette. As far as I know, she's still sleeping with Bob Rodgers, who I sometimes see waiting on line at Caldwell's.

In a way, Bob Rodgers is much more attractive than Howard and I can almost understand why Annette would gravitate from one to the other, although why Bob Rodgers would be interested in her is another question.

Already the days when Howard and I could barely keep our hands off one another on the way to the motel are fading into memory. Often, we don't say a word from the time we leave the parking lot to the time we reach the motel. It's only fifteen miles but feels longer, like we've been sentenced to life in prison for all our crimes, no time off for good behavior.

Howard is always angry and I try to steer clear of any topics that might lead to a confrontation. And since all topics seem particularly loaded these days, I'm better off saying nothing.

"What are you angry about?"

In the old days I used to secretly wish that I would get pregnant with Howard's baby. Now I wait nervously for my period to come and mark off the days on a calendar to make sure I'm not late.

—Howard is furious whenever I go out with Eduardo.

At first I tried to temper his anger by saying Eduardo meant nothing to me and that the only reason I was doing it was so my parents would stop worrying about me.

"My father wants me to go see a shrink and if he knows I'm going out with someone I won't have to." If my parents found out I was seeing Howard they'd probably lock me up somewhere.

I realize that I'm better off not telling Howard how often I see Eduardo (I should never have told him I was seeing him in the first place) but I'm frightened that if I lie to him he'll find out anyway.

Eduardo stops by on his way to school in the morning and we walk up the hill together. It's almost a half-mile and I let him hold my hand. Everyone in school knows we're going out together and it's a relief not to feel so secretive. When I tell Howard I have no feelings for Eduardo I'm not telling the truth, though we haven't done anything except kiss good night.

The fact that we've seen each other so frequently without touching only makes me desire him more. I have the feeling that Eduardo might be offended if I make a pass at him and though I admire his self-control it also makes me a little sick.

I'm tempted to ask if he's not attracted to me, if he doesn't want to kiss me—for a reason I don't know about—but I don't have the nerve.

—My mother no longer wears a bra. Her breasts float free under her sweaters and blouses with none of the ambiguity and restraint that a bra imposes. You can see her nipples straining against the fabric. I wonder what the people she meets at work think about her appearance, if anyone even notices.

Probably women can tell the difference more than men; the men just wonder why they never noticed this attractive woman before. It makes a trip to the bank more pleasurable if the person giving you your money is attractive and good natured. I date this change in my mother's appearance to the start of her affair with Bud Chaffin, the owner of the East Winston Nursery.

She and Bud go out almost every night. Often, I'm asleep when she gets back. I don't hear her come in. And then the next morning I make coffee and bring it to her in bed. Some mornings I have to force her to get up; she looks groggy, drugged, hung over. Other mornings she's downstairs before I am: refreshed, eager to begin her day.

All she seems interested in is buying new clothes and makeup. One day, after school, she asks me if I want to go shopping with her. We drive into town and stop in front of The Lemon Tree. We try on skirts and scarves and expensive blouses trimmed with sequins and beads.

It's been a long time since I've seen my mother so happy. (I notice, as we take off our clothes, that she no longer wears underpants either.)

—Sometimes when Howard and I make love I close my eyes and pretend I'm making love to Ted. Afterwards, I feel guilty and act overly affectionate to him.

No doubt Ted and Annette would be a perfect pair. Neither of them has much interest in anyone's body but their own.

—Before I go to sleep I think about Eduardo Narcimento. I carry on imaginary conversations with him in my head.

"Did you have any girlfriends in Mexico City?" I ask.

Howard calls me late at night, when Annette's asleep or with her lover, and forces me to talk about the future, "our" future as he puts it. He acts as if nothing's changed between us. "Well," I say, baiting him, "when are you going to leave Annette?"

At the Acorn Acres I lie on top of the bed just like before, my clothing scattered on the floor, and let him do what he likes, but my heart isn't there.

—I'm not in love with Howard, I'm in love with Eduardo, I hate Ted. I love Howard, I'm not in love with Eduardo, I hate Ted. I love, I hate.

"I've never slept with Eduardo." Howard thinks I'm being unfaithful to him (I don't care what he thinks). "I love you," I say, but I know I don't mean it. And he knows it too.

"Eduardo really likes you," Susan Assuado tells me. Eduardo's living in a room in her house. Susan's father,

Manny, is the coach of the track team. I wonder why Susan and Eduardo don't get together.

I think that Howard hates me. He hates all women. Some nights I wake up suddenly with a great craving to be with Ted. I say his name aloud in the dark. I have to cancel out whole memories, literally cross them out with two thick strokes of an imaginary magic marker, in order to get through the day. I wonder if I made a mistake by breaking up with Ted.

Everyone has faults and problems; no one's perfect, including myself.

Ed Plank, the referee, tossed Billie the ball. She balanced it between her fingers and studied it without seeing it, fitting the seams to her palms, bounced it once, paused, turned it over, bounced it again, wiped the sweat from her forehead with the back of her arm.

She stared defiantly into the crowd of faces ogling her behind the backboard: you can wave and shout all you want, you jerks, but nothing's going to distract me. Out of the corner of one eye she caught a glimpse of the opposing team's coach, Kevin Hawkings, kneeling in front of the Carmel bench in his three-piece suit, buttoned down shirt and tie.

"Clean block," he was shouting, implying that Debbie Pilute, the girl guarding Billie, had hit the ball, not Billie's hand as the referee claimed.

The fans clutching their bed sheets with the words "Carmel #1" or merely "We're Number 1" painted on them, took up the cheer—"clean block! clean block!"—stomping their feet against the wooden brackets of the dilapidated bleachers until the sound reverberated off the walls of the gym and made Billie feel like she was standing in the eye of a vortex where all the demons and angels, living and dead, were calling her name.

Susan Assuado, one of the three Susans on the East Winston team, came up behind Billie and patted her on the ass. It was part of the ritual: when Susan went to the foul line, it was Billie who slapped her ass and whispered a few words of encouragement to calm her down.

Billie knew, and Debbie Pilute knew, as well, that the referee had been justified in calling the foul. Debbie and her coach could argue forever and Ed Plank, who managed a bowling alley in Pittsfield and was probably in better shape than most of the girls (he ran five miles every morning before going to work) wouldn't change his mind.

It was the start of the last quarter, the score was tied, every point counted—and arguing, even if you knew you were wrong, was part of the game. Maybe next time there was a close call the referee would give you the benefit of the doubt.

It had been a disappointing season, to say the least. East Winston had lost its opening game to Monument Mountain by twenty points on the night of the season's first blizzard (not only did they lose but they had to suffer the indignity of sleeping over on the floor of their opponent's gym), their second by fifteen points to the Holyoke Wildcats starring Barbara Mahoney, at 6'3" the tallest woman player in the county, and their third to Springfield Latin, the worst team in the league, by ten. There was little solace in the fact that they were losing by less each game since they'd begun the season with high expectations and even Coach Miller, cautious by nature, had predicted a county championship.

"I think we have the talent to go all the way," she announced before the season started, not in any sexual sense where "all the way" might mean that the entire East Winston team was now talented enough to make love, but "all the way" to the state finals in Boston.

Billie, as team captain, blamed herself for the lack of success, and after they lost their first five games suggested that Margie Rappaport, a sophomore, take her place in the starting lineup. It couldn't hurt, and maybe the team would have more luck with Billie coming off the bench. But the plan backfired, the other team took advantage of Margie's inexperience on defense, and by the time Billie entered the game East Winston was too far behind to catch up.

As captain, Billie felt she should be providing inspiration, if nothing else, but instead she spent most of her energy trying to camouflage the fact that she couldn't care less whether the team won or lost.

The residue of her friendship with Ted was still in the air, and Billie supposed her teammates credited her desultory play to her "personal problems."

But if she has so many problems, some of them felt, maybe she shouldn't be playing at all. She didn't feel particularly sullen or unhappy, just indifferent, a shadow of some other person she could only half-remember.

Billie wondered if professional athletes were advised to abstain from sex before a game. She and Howard had switched their "day" from Monday to Friday, and most of the games were scheduled for Friday and Saturday nights. She couldn't believe that any athlete would remain celibate for an entire season, or that not having sex would make him or her a better player. Did sex dull the desire to win? Even Howard was concerned that he was the reason Billie was playing so poorly. It was their private joke, something to laugh about in the shadows of Room 19 at the Acorn Acres.

The men's basketball team was doing better than ever and Ted had blossomed into a true star at last. Billie had assumed that he'd do something destructive as a way of making her feel guilty for ending their relationship. Instead, she heard rumors that he'd stopped drinking and that he was even planning to go to college but no one knew, or would tell her, the reason for this sudden change.

If nothing else, Billie missed discussing basketball with him, how to set a pick or block out your defensive person when you went up for a rebound. She'd probably learned more from him about the game than he'd learned from her about writing papers, or at least as much.

About once a week they passed one another in the hall, said hello, but never stopped to talk, and once Billie saw him from a distance with his arm around the shoulder of another girl, a sophomore named Gerry who had recently moved to the area from the Midwest and who had short black hair and heavy silver loops dangling from her ears and was wearing a long black straight skirt with a gold belt and an orange turtleneck. It was Billie's impression, more a rationalization than anything else, that she wasn't Ted's type, not aware that for the first time in her life she was experiencing real jealousy.

Susan Barrett, the tallest girl on the East Winston team, stood on the edge of the foul line, her arms in the air. Before the game she'd asked Billie for a tampax.

"If you see any blood on the floor you'll know it's mine." (She was joking, but such things were known to happen.)

Billie was expecting her own period any day and had a new unopened box of tampax in her locker. She was a week late and the thought that she might be pregnant was yet another distraction; the ultimate one, in a sense, everything else faded in comparison. How could you care about basketball when you were going to have a baby?

"I'm late," she told Howard the last time they made love, but he didn't act worried or seem anxious to talk about it. Maybe he wants me to get pregnant so he'll have an excuse to leave Annette? Billie knew about five girls in her class who had had abortions, including Nicky, and there was no reason why Billie couldn't get one too: her parents wouldn't even have to know.

Howard often said that he wanted more children. More babies. "Now that Emma and Sara are growing up I miss having a real baby around."

A real baby meant someone who was totally dependent on you for everything. Billie wasn't sure she was ready to take care of another human being, though having a child and living with Howard in a place where they didn't know anyone was part of a recurring fantasy which invaded her daydreams and made the future, her plans for the future, as real as anything happening in the present: certainly more real than trying to toss a ball into a net.

Susan Barrett had beautiful legs which she shaved with a disposable razor in the locker room before every game. She had a boyfriend in college who often picked her up after school in his used Mercedes when he was in town and who always sent her a single red rose in a long narrow box before each game. She sat in front of her locker, blissful, staring at the flower as if it were more than a symbol of her boyfriend's love but could actually speak in his place and say the words "I love you" aloud.

East Winston and Carmel had played together earlier in the year and Carmel had won easily. Carmel was having its troubles too (one of the starting players had been arrested for selling heroin in the cafeteria and Kevin Hawkings kept threatening to quit and take a job coaching in college) but had somehow managed to win twice as many games as East Winston.

Before the game, the East Winston players had sat in a circle in the locker room cursing out the Carmel players, their arch rivals. The competition between the teams had grown ugly during the last few years. By an unwritten law, dating between the schools was forbidden, and if you were an East Winston girl you risked being ostracized by your classmates if you dared to go out with a guy from Carmel.

"I'm going to kick Debbie Pilute's ass," Billie said, trying to psyche herself up before the game.

It wasn't only the last game of the year but the last game of her career as a high school basketball player. The colleges she had applied to (Smith, Sarah Lawrence, Brown, Barnard) probably didn't even have women's basketball teams.

Going off to college, leaving East Winston, "the future"—she wanted to discuss these things with Howard, but he never seemed interested.

"We still have time," he would say, patting her back in a way that made Billie feel he was patronizing her, that in his eyes she was still too young to have to worry about the problems of real life. It was painful for her to realize that being together with another person was more dependent on practical matters like school and jobs than her own feelings.

"I decided I'm going to leave Annette."

They were lying in bed in their room at the Acorn Acres. Locked inside, behind the layers of dusty venetian blinds and yellow plastic curtains. Hidden beneath the quilts, side by side, Howard's hand resting on the inside of her thigh. Lying in bed, in a cocoon, a womb. "A love-nest." Soon it would be time to leave, to walk back into their lives and pretend that nothing mattered except schoolwork, basketball, other people's marital problems and taxes.

"But what if I go to school in New York?"

"I'll get a job there. Don't worry."

"Can Emma and Sara come with us?"

Annette didn't care whether anyone knew about her affair with Bob Rodgers, not even his wife.

"Where do they meet?" Billie wanted to know.

Howard didn't seem to mind discussing his wife's infidelities and Billie was curious about how people she knew, people who weren't merely characters in novels but living flesh and blood, conducted their lives.

Were all adults—she hedged about including herself in such a category—as stupid as her parents? As Howard and Annette?

"When she first started seeing him or when I figured out she was seeing someone I followed her one morning before going to work. It bothers me a lot less if I know for certain that she's having an affair. It's the doubting and all the anxiety that goes along with wondering what's happening, with not knowing what's happening, that I can't stand.

"Though at this point there isn't much Annette's going to do that's going to affect me. Rodgers lives in that new housing complex off Monument Valley Road. It's supposed to attract single people and young couples though I think half the apartments are still empty. The Rodgers moved in right after it opened. They even bought an apartment there—"

"I know the place you mean," Billie said.

Monument Mansions had been a source of controversy since the day the spokesman from Tyler Corporation in Boston had stood up in front of the town planning commission and proposed the idea of converting the swamp land and forest area off Monument Valley Road into a place where younger couples, unable to afford their own homes, could live, raise families and feel they were permanent members of the community.

"Well she got out of her car, she just parked it right in front of Rodgers' house, she didn't park it down the street from the house but practically in the driveway, and went upstairs to his place. A minute after she entered the building I saw this hand reach out and draw the curtains on the windows facing the road."

Howard turned his palms upwards and shrugged as if to say that what happened after that wasn't his business.

"The first time I found out she was sleeping with someone, after Emma and Sara were born, was the worst. I even began to wonder whether Emma and Sara were my kids. Whether I was their father. They look like me, I think, at least people say they do. Though maybe they're just being polite. People say that about everybody's babies. She looks just like you. She has your chin. Anyway, I made Annette swear she hadn't fucked anyone but me around the time she got pregnant, even though I knew that if she had been fucking someone else she wouldn't tell me anyway.

"Her first lover had once been a close friend of mine and that had made it all doubly painful and for awhile I didn't know who to blame. Him, Annette, myself. But now I don't blame myself anymore. And I don't even feel like hitting Annette—which is what I did after the first time."

"What do you mean 'hit'?" Billie asked, staring at his hands.

There was a spot in the center of the backboard, a few inches above the rim, which she always aimed at when she went to the foul line. Nineteen times out of twenty, if she hit that imaginary square, the ball went in. It was only when she thought too much about what she was doing, aimed too carefully, that she missed. She was the best foul shooter on the team and her ability at the free throw line was what caught Coach Miller's attention in gym class early in Billie's sophomore year.

"You should try out for the team," the coach had told her.

Those early weeks of practice had been torture. What she remembered most was the ladder of pain extending from under her right arm to the top of her thigh which felt like a new appendage had attached itself to her body and was nourishing itself and would never go away; the taste of salt on the tip of her tongue as the sweat rolled down the sides of her face and the tip of her nose like rain down the side of an awning; the throbbing in her upper arms when she woke in the morning and literally hauled herself out of bed into the bathroom where even brushing her teeth was a minor ordeal; the sound of Coach Miller's whistle which meant practice was over for the day and which was greeted by a collective sigh of relief as the members of the team paraded into the locker room, stripped off their uniforms and stood under the shower; and, more than anything else, the feeling of camaraderie—Billie had never liked being part of a group before and was surprised that she was accepted so readily, even by the seniors, and that it was easy to fit in without losing one's identity—as they traded lipsticks, combed out the knots from each other's hair, and talked about their boyfriends in a way that made Billie blush and wonder whether any of her new friends would be surprised if she told them she was still a virgin.

As soon as she took the shot Billie knew it wasn't going to go in. ("I just threw up a brick," she said to Howard the next day.)

"No!" she shouted, while the ball was still in the air, hoping Barrett and Assuado, closest to the basket, would hear her voice and leap for the rebound.

She saw the four bodies merge under the backboard and was tempted to join in, but Debbie Pilute, who Ted once called "the best woman player I've ever seen," had boxed out both East Winston girls.

Though Debbie was a guard, she had extraordinary vertical leap from a standing position and could usually out rebound girls who were a half foot taller. The ball bounced directly off the backboard without even touching the net but Debbie was there to clear it easily. Billie began backpedaling, slowly, as the other girls raced by. It was her job to guard Debbie as she brought the ball up court.

Debbie dribbled along the sidelines, taking her time, walking the ball past the East Winston bench. Billie greeted her at mid court, her arms in the air.

Howard was sitting behind the bench, a few rows back, sipping black coffee from a styrofoam cup. He came to every home game and always sat in the same place but Billie never looked in his direction when she was on the court.

"I used to play a little ball myself," he explained, vaguely, to the parents of the other girls who were surprised at his devotion to the girl's team but who accepted his presence after awhile ("There's Howard

Ryan again," they would whisper when he took his seat) and assumed that he just wanted to escape from his life with Annette, whose reputation in town had become a bit of a legend, and that he didn't have any designs on one of their daughters (little did they know). Howard once suggested to Billie that he drive her home after the game but she vetoed the idea for fear that being seen in public together in any way would arouse suspicion.

"I don't care if anyone knows," Howard said.

"But I do. As long as you're married to Annette...."

The first step involved extricating himself from his marriage and working out an arrangement where he could see his kids as much as possible, if not live with them a good deal of the time. If they ever had to go to court, Annette's reputation would probably work against her, though there was no proof that having lovers, being an unfaithful wife, didn't mean you couldn't be a good mother.

Billie occasionally wondered if she shouldn't take a year off from school so she and Howard could resettle somewhere, so she could devote herself to him and the kids. Then, once they'd made all the transitions, she could begin dealing with her own needs.

The thought that she might be pregnant was scary—during classes she made lists of names for an imaginary daughter: Francesca, Violet, Crystal, Mimi and Jeanette were her favorites—but it wasn't the worst thing that could happen.

She couldn't imagine two people more dissimilar than Howard and Mitch. What would they say to one another if they ever met?

Howard had long ago lost the habit of reading for pleasure and in an attempt to encourage him Billie found herself playing the role of tutor once again.

"Here, read this," she handed him a copy of *Great Expectations*, the same copy she had given to Ted.

Mitch hated lawyers on principal; no doubt Howard would have to convince him that he wasn't like all the others.

Howard spent his free time building models of dinosaurs in the basement of his house. They were made of unstained wood and came in a kit. He glued together the pieces according to the instructions, much the same way he had put together model airplanes as a child. "It's my only hobby," he admitted, feeling a bit insecure, since Billie's curiosity about everything could be a little formidable at times.

Besides reading, Mitch enjoyed listening to opera. In the closet at home Billie once found a shoe box filled with old playbills, momentos from the time her parents first began dating, for *La Traviata*, *La Boheme*, *Don Giovanni*.

"He used to have crushes on all the mezzos," Chris once said. "He'd drag me along even if there were no seats and make me stand behind the orchestra."

Rainy Saturday afternoons Mitch spent in front of the fire listening to *The Marriage of Figaro* or *Rigoletto* on his earphones.

Neither Mitch nor Howard had any close male friends. "At a certain age men have a harder time trusting one another than women do."

That was Chris's theory, anyway. That's why men get together and play poker one night a week or go hunting together. They enjoy each other's company as long as they're doing something competitive. Most men don't even dream of just getting together and talking. Both Howard and Mitch liked to drink and Howard wasn't adverse to going to a bar now and then and hanging out for a few hours. Billie was surprised, though, when he told her, as they drove back to town from the motel, that his favorite bar was The Willows, the tavern where Ted had taken her on their first date.

"Do you know Whip?"

It was Howard's turn to look surprised.

"You mean you've been there?"

"Just once. My old boyfriend Ted, the one I told you about, took me."

Debbie Pilute's major flaw was her unwillingness to pass the ball.

She brought it up court, dribbled, ignoring her teammates. This time she faked a pass and when Billie went for the steal Debbie dribbled around her.

As Susan Assuado and Hannah Mulwork converged, waving their arms to help out, she passed off to the Carmel center who was open and easily scored.

"Fuck you," Debbie hissed in Billie's ear as she glided down the court.

Carmel was ahead by three now, but there were still eight minutes to go. As Billie took the ball at the baseline, she looked over to the bench to see whether Coach Miller was planning to call a time out. The coach caught Billie's eye and moved her hand in the shuffling gesture which meant that Billie should speed things up. Billie was exhausted, she had played the whole game, but figured the coach wanted to save the time outs (each team was allowed three time outs per half) for the closing minutes.

Mitch had attended most of the home games during Billie's sophomore year but had stopped coming in any regular way for fear that he might meet Chris who often showed up at the spur of the moment, usually with a few of her girlfriends, on nights when they had nothing better to do. Billie didn't encourage her parents to come, though she had hoped that her success as a basketball player would bring them together in some small way rather than distance them even further. Joanne, though she often promised to come to the games, had never seen her play. She was taller than Billie and would have made a good basketball player herself.

"I just never had any interest in sports," she said.

Both Mitch and Chris, as well as Joanne, were all sedentary types, who (if they had the choice) would spend most of their days at home, sitting in a chair at a desk or in front of a fire, lying in bed under thick quilts, head propped on pillows, book in hand.

Howard was similar; one reason he hadn't left Annette was that it required too much energy. It was easier to go through life suffering moderately than to make any major change which might involve the eventual freedom from suffering but which, along the way, might also involve experiencing an extreme form of pain that he didn't yet know about. For Howard, a lifetime of moderate suffering was preferable to an occasional interval of extreme pain. At least that's the way he'd felt before meeting Billie.

She flipped the ball to Susan Leaf and jogged down court. There was Debbie Pilute, waiting for her, a few feet beyond the mid-court line.

Susan Leaf had the largest breasts of any of the players on the East Winston team and had to wear a special support bra which she ordered from a store in Boston. On a bus ride home, late one night, she confessed to Billie that she'd had a secret crush on Ted for the last three years.

"If you don't mind my asking, what's he like in bed?"

"You can have him," Billie said. She wanted to tell Susan Leaf that she wasn't Ted's type but didn't want to say anything that would hurt her friend's feelings.

Susan never wore any makeup and tended to favor baggy pants and sweaters (Billie couldn't remember ever seeing her in a dress or skirt) which made her look even bigger than she was. On the other hand, Susan might be perfect for Ted, who seemed to take pleasure in telling women how much makeup they should wear and how to dress. At least the old Ted, the Ted Billie remembered, the person he was when he was with me ("keep your skirt on") was like that.

As they crossed the mid-court line Susan handed her the ball. As soon as she started dribbling Debbie Pilute reached out and hit her hand but this time Ed Plank didn't notice.

Billie scowled at her, passed off again to Susan Leaf who held the ball for less than a second before passing it in the opposite direction to Susan Assuado who passed it without a pause to the center, Susan Barrett, who threw it out to Billie again.

Debbie Pilute knew that Billie was going to take the shot and leapt in her face following the general trajectory of Billie's body as it arched away from her defender so that she seemed to be falling backwards as the ball left her hands. Debbie Pilute could have kept her balance but instead let her momentum carry her in Billie's direction as if she were making a jackknife dive and the wooden floor of the gym was a pool of water so that a moment after Billie hit the floor Debbie fell also, landing crosswise, the toes of her sneakers hitting Billie's ribs.

Debbie rolled to one side, away from Billie, and got to her feet almost immediately without even looking over her shoulder to see whether Billie was hurt.

It was obvious that she was hurt; a collective silence spread over the gym as she writhed on the floor, clutching her side where Debbie had kicked her. Susan Barrett, who had seen it all, grabbed Debbie Pilute by the arms, swung her around and slapped her across the face with her open palm. Debbie responded by lashing out with her fists but her blow glanced off Susan's shoulder as she backed away. By the time Debbie Pilute had a chance to throw another punch Coach Miller had stepped in behind her and grabbed both her arms while one of the Carmel reserves restrained Susan Barrett.

The trainer of the East Winston team, Harry Bowa, knelt at her side.

"Calm down," he said, taking her hand, "you'll be O.K."

His voice was low and sexy, and seemed to be coming from the end of a tunnel, beyond the lights at the top of the gym which were swimming through a mist of tears like a string of lanterns reflected in water. Where was Ted and Eduardo? Why didn't Howard do something?

"She didn't have to fall! She kicked me! Didn't anyone see it?"

Billie felt the bump where her head had hit the floor. It seemed to be growing larger as she touched it.

"We'll put some ice on that and take a few x-rays of those ribs."

Harry Bowa spoke with a thick Southern accent. He was in his fifties and had lived in East Winston for twenty years but because of his accent people still thought of him as an "outsider."

"Let's get you into the locker room."

Billie tightened her hold on his hand and let him hoist her into a standing position. Her back was stiff, her side was throbbing, but at least she could walk. She put one arm around Harry Bowa's shoulder and another arm around Coach Miller's waist and walked slowly to the bench.

The East Winston cheerleaders, in red and white striped skirts and shiny red underwear and red leotards with the letters EW on the back, stood along the sidelines like a troupe of clowns. Debbie Pilute sat under the basket shouting at Ed Plank who stared, with dismay, at the coffee cups, beer cans and candy wrappers which the irate Carmel students had tossed onto the court. He approached Kevin Hawkings, the Carmel coach, and told him that he would cancel the game unless the coach was able to restrain his players and fans, but Hawkings just threw up his hands as if it wasn't his business. If Ed wanted to stop the game that was fine with him.

As Milton Warwick, the Carmel high school custodian, began mopping up the debris, an empty beer can flew from somewhere in the stands and struck him on the forehead. Harry Bowa returned to the court, poured a tumbler's worth of antiseptic over the wound and covered it with a gauze bandage. Everyone in the gym was standing except for Howard Ryan who had spilled coffee over his pants when he saw Billie hit the floor and was blotting the stains with a napkin which Esta Assuado, Susan's mother, had given him

"I wanted to go out onto the court and do something...."

It was 1 P.M., a few days after the game, and they were driving in the blue Cadillac to the room at the Acorn Acres.

"I'm glad you didn't. It would have only made things worse."

"What I wanted to do was shoot that coach."

"The creep," Billie said, as they pulled into the motel parking lot, "isn't worth shooting."

She had spent the day after the game in bed at her mother's with a hot water bottle on her ribs and an ice pack on her forehead. She tried to read but Debbie Pilute's face kept flickering on the edge of her thoughts, the maniacal expression as she floated like a kamikaze pilot through mid-air. She couldn't understand why Debbie hated her so much.

She would doze off for awhile, talk on the phone, swallow a few spoonfuls of chicken broth, and go back to sleep. Her father called and made a crack about her last game and how she was going out "With a bang" and Eduardo called and sent her a bouquet of baby roses and Nicky called as a gesture of peace which Billie accepted without saying anything about their fight and even the East Winston high school principal called to tell her he was going to make a formal protest to the Massachusetts High School Athletic Association about Kevin Hawkings' behavior during the game.

Billie's ribs were still sore and the last thing she felt like doing was making love. She had tried to put Howard off but he had insisted on seeing her and as usual it was hard for Billie to say no. She couldn't understand how people could be so selfish. What she wanted most was to lie in a hot bath and close her eyes, stay in bed for a week and read *The Magic Mountain* or *Our Mutual Friend*, a novel that went on forever. She wished she could inspire Howard to read more books so they could have more to talk about. She was sick of hearing about his problems with Annette. She had given him *Tender is the Night* and *Madame Bovary* but whenever she asked him about the books he said: "I don't have time."

But what about at night, she wanted to ask. She couldn't believe that he spent all his time in the basement putting together his stupid model dinosaurs.

Not having enough time wasn't a good excuse; no one had time, but that didn't mean things didn't get done. If you want to do something you'll do it, you'll make time. It was obvious that Howard just wasn't interested in reading the books.

There was something pitiable about the image of Annette going out and sleeping with other men while Howard stayed home gluing together tiny bits of wood and the more Billie got to know Howard the more sympathy and understanding she felt for Annette. If I were married to Howard, she thought, I'd sleep around as well.

Howard liked to talk to her about the past, about growing up in Indiana. His childhood, his family. His mother had died when he was five and his father had remarried shortly after. Then his father died and he lived for awhile with his stepmother and her kids from her first marriage until she married someone else.

"But by then I'd gotten a scholarship to go off to school."

They all lived in a small cinder block house on the outskirts of Indianapolis.

"My stepmother's new husband drank alot and we were on welfare most of the time. I remember lying awake late at night listening to them fighting."

He had met Annette during his sophomore year at college. He remembered the first night he saw her; it was the year she'd been voted Hog Queen and had a thousand other boyfriends. She was sitting across from him at a table in the cafeteria and as they were introduced she took his hand and batted her eyelashes and made Howard feel that if he could think of the right words to say she would be his, she would be his slave, she would go off with him and do anything.

In the early days, when Billie and Howard first began sleeping together, she used to interrupt him with a million different questions about the past. Did you and Annette make love on your first date? Were you a virgin? Was she? But now she used the time after making love, when Howard liked to talk about himself, to imagine what it would be like to be in bed with Eduardo Narcimento. While Howard droned on, lost in the intricacies of his past, oblivious to whether she was listening to him or not.

Early evening, mid-April, and Billie was sitting at her desk reading *Middlemarch*, her elbows propped in old sliced lemons to smooth the elephant skin, when Chris, wearing a white knee-length dress with a full pleated skirt and the opal teardrop earrings Billie had bought her last Christmas, pushed open the door of the room and announced that she was going out for the night.

"You look pretty," Billie said. "Where did you get that dress?"

"I'll tell you tomorrow, I'm in a rush." She spun around quickly so that her dress flared around her thighs and blew Billie a kiss. "Don't wait up."

Billie's windows faced the front of the house. She heard the sound of her mother's low heels scraping the stone path leading down to the street, the hum of the engine as the car pulled away from the curb.

Billie's first thought was to call Eduardo and invite him over but they had a date the following night and she worried that they might get bored if they saw each other too frequently.

She wondered where Chris was going and why she was acting so mysteriously. Ever since the afternoon Billie came home early from school and saw Mitch's car parked out front she'd suspected that her parents had become lovers. Just last week she arrived home to find Chris and Mitch sitting round the kitchen table drinking beer, mid-afternoon, and eating salted pretzels out of a bag. Mitch had his legs propped on a chair and was telling Chris the story of an old "Twilight Zone" episode which he'd recently seen. The light was streaming through the lavender curtains making shadowy patterns on the red and white checkered tablecloth. Chris stared at her former husband, attentive, beaming, remembering the time when they used to watch "Twilight Zone" reruns late at night. Sometimes Billie would crawl into bed with them; more often they would make love before the show ended and fall asleep in each other's arms with the TV still going.

Her hair was pulled back under a blue scarf which curved over the top of her head like a visor. She was wearing a pink and white check gingham apron with straps that crossed in the back over dungarees and a blue work shirt. The light floated through the beer in the thin stemmed glasses. The head of foam in the glass Billie poured for herself pulsated in the glow. Billie loved being in the same room with both her parents. It was like heaven.

Last weekend she'd stayed over at Mitch's house, like always, but Joanne hadn't been there.

"She's visiting some friends in New York," was Mitch's explanation.

When Billie asked him how long she was going to be gone he shrugged and tried to change the subject. Billie checked out Joanne's closet and saw that it was almost half-empty. And her jewelry box: all the earrings and necklaces were gone. The rings with Nepalese stones. The lapis necklace from Guatamela.

Joanne's absence permeated the house. Mitch cloistered himself in his room and only came out to prepare meals. Billie tried not to link Joanne's departure with the image of her father and mother sitting around the table, but it was hard to avoid the connection. Just when you get used to an arrangement something happens (in this case, the thing Billie least expected), and the whole process of adaptation, acclimation and adjustment begins again.

"Why are men so stupid?" Chris asked, the morning after she went out on her date.

"They're not all stupid."

Billie was trying to be positive, though she hardly considered herself an authority on the subject of what all men were like. Chris looked exhausted; she had deep circles under her eyes and barely enough energy to pour herself a cup of coffee.

"Do you want to talk?"

"I'm too tired to talk," she said. "Right now I don't even know if there's anything to talk about."

"Why don't you call the bank and tell them you're sick. You look sick."

"I'm not sick, just tired. I'm not used to staying out this late."

"Get into bed and I'll give you a back rub. Bring you some tea."

"What about school?"

"Fuck school. I can go later."

"I hate it when you say 'fuck'."

"I hate it when you think it's important whether I say it or not."

Though Billie had managed to keep Howard a secret from her parents for almost six months, she couldn't understand why they were keeping secrets from her. She was no longer babysitting for the Ryans but was still seeing Howard. They met every Friday at 12:30 in the parking lot behind the library and drove, like always, to their room at the Acorn Acres. But it was all different now—at least she felt different— and was having trouble faking even the barest trace of emotion.

Whenever Howard talked about Annette and how he was going to leave her, Billie closed her eyes and thought about Eduardo, what it would be like to make love to him. She pictured him racing around the track behind the high school, full speed, while his coach, Manny Assuado, stood on the sidelines with a stop watch. She wanted to tell Howard that she didn't care whether he left Annette or not but she couldn't bear to say it, she was afraid of what he might do.

She stood, fully dressed, in the bathroom of the motel, staring at herself in the mirror, when Howard came up behind her and lifted her skirt.

"I don't want to," she said, as he pressed against her. "I have a lot of work to do today. Drive me home."

"I saw Annette Ryan last night," Chris said. They were upstairs in Chris's bedroom, in what had once been her parents' bedroom, and Billie was rubbing coconut oil into her mother's back. "Remember her?"

"How could I forget?"

"She was at this party, but she wasn't with her husband. Apparently she's been having an affair with this guy named Bob Rodgers. Her husband knows about it, his wife knows about it. No one paid much attention but I was appalled. She couldn't keep her hands off him, not for a minute. Even he looked a little embarrassed."

Billie pushed the weight of her palms against Chris's ribs. If she was ever going to tell her mother about her affair with Howard, now was the time.

"She's a lot prettier than I thought, that's one thing. And she doesn't seem to be drinking that much, or so people say. But her voice! How can anyone stand listening to it for more than five minutes?"

"You can fuck without talking," Billie said.

"Is that what you like to do?"

She was standing in the bathroom at the Acorn Acres, putting on lipstick, when Howard came up behind her. He lifted her skirt and put his hand between her legs.

"Don't," she said, twisting away. "I feel sore.'

She tried to say it in a good humored way, in a way that wouldn't make Howard feel he was being rejected, but it was hard for her to hide the contempt in her voice. He didn't insist.

"I'll wait for you in the car," he said, letting the screen door slam into place.

There was still pleasure in making love to him but it was pleasure tainted by absence of feeling so that only part of her was ever truly with him while the other part was looking on like an angel floating in the shadows of the ceiling and still another part of her was carrying on a dialogue in her head with Eduardo. Sometimes she'd open her eyes when they were making love and Howard would be staring at her as if he were trying to read her mind and find out where she'd gone.

*

April 15

Dear Eduardo,

(1 AM) having just left you & already I want to say I MISS YOU! Do you mind? Mind my saying it & mind my writing this to you.

I want to write to you—it's better than talking to you in my head (which I do endlessly) or writing about you in my diary, or, sometimes, talking to you on the phone. I love to hear your voice but it's frustrating and just makes me want to be with you even more. I can't believe we have to wait a whole week before we can go out—seeing each other at school is fun, but not the same thing. We need hours together—sometimes it takes me about an hour before I even feel comfortable when I'm with you—I feel so nervous whenever we go out like maybe you won't like the way I look or that you might not even show up (I'm not usually insecure, I've just never been in love).

I wish you felt free to tell me everything you're thinking—even negative things, what you don't like about me—I want to know everything that's going on in your heart and mind. You're so reserved (I don't mean that as a criticism—I realize it's the way you were brought up) compared to most of the other guys I know—and I dare say, as the English might say, it's the reason I like you so much.

Maybe writing letters (this is a hint) might be a good way of practicing your English—and I don't mean that as a criticism either but you've told me you wanted help and actually putting into words what you're feeling is the best way (maybe) to do it. Everyone's so fucking self-conscious, don't you think?

(After all this, if you don't write me I'll be angry.)

Now, since you're not here to rock me to sleep, I'm trying to read myself into submission but the book is too boring to even put me to sleep—It's called Middlemarch *and it was written by a woman—a woman—named George Eliot. Her real name was Mary Anne Evans but she was frightened that people wouldn't read her book if they knew the author was a woman. At least that's what my father told me. (There was another writer in the 19th century, a French woman, who also called herself George—George Sand—but I haven't read any of her books and I don't know her real name.) My real name isn't Billie and I hesitate to tell you what it is but if I ever write a book I'm not going to call myself Bill or George. (Do you have a middle name?) (I do, but I can't tell you that either.)*

I want to go to Mexico with you. My father told me about a place called Yucatan where they have a lot of Mayan ruins. He (and Joanne, his wife) have been everywhere, though there's something going on between them recently that's been a bit upsetting to me. She's in New York City "visiting a friend" but I fear she's never coming back (most of her clothing and jewelry are gone). My father's been very mysterious and very grouchy about everything.

He and my mother are getting along well and for awhile I thought that they were having an affair but I guess it was just wishful thinking on my part.

My mother's going out with this guy named Bud who works in the nursery, I think he's one of the owners, but I'm not sure I like him. He treats me like I'm a little kid even though he's only eight years older than I am! My mother seems happier than she's been in years so I can't complain but I'm also afraid that she's going to get hurt. Bud's practically the only guy she's gone out with more than once since she and my father split up.

I know that older men like younger women so there's no reason why older women shouldn't dig younger men, too, but my instinct tells me that Bud isn't the type who's going to stay with any one woman for too long. My instinct isn't infallible but I'm a pretty good judge of human nature (at least I think I am).

I always think I've grown accustomed to the idea that my parents don't live together and then suddenly I'm shocked into realizing how much it all means to me. I can understand rationally how two people can get married and have a child or lots of children and stop loving one another but I can't help feeling like I've been ignored and that they might have figured out a way of honoring that initial feeling between them which resulted in giving birth to me!

I know that compared to what happened to you I should be grateful that my parents still live in the same town and that I can see either of them whenever I want, and I know they both still love me—I've never doubted that. Yet I'm always on the brink of expectation—like each day something new might happen and my father or mother might suddenly announce they're getting back together again or that one of them's moving to California or something and whatever they say I just have to nod my head as if anything they did was OK with me. Some days I feel like I'm their parents and that they need my help and support more than I need them. Do you know what I mean?

I wish we could travel together—send me a list of all the places you've never been that you'd like to visit. I've never been anywhere. High on my list would be a trip to Nepal so I could stand in the foothills of Mount Everest. I wish you could sneak out of your little prison and come see me right now. I wish this book by this strange woman named George wasn't so boring. I miss you, once again, your love,

B.

*

When Billie returned home from school the thick envelopes were waiting on the inside mat where the mail person, Astrid Peterson, had dropped them through the slot in the door earlier that morning. Three of the envelopes were from colleges she had applied to: Brown, Smith, Barnard. The fourth envelope, she could tell by the handwriting, was from Eduardo Narcimento.

She sat at the kitchen table, amid the squares and patches of light and shadow, and stared at the envelopes. Then she opened them, one by one, using her thumbnail to tear a hole down the side. Each of the letters—"We are happy to inform you...."—began the same way.

She thought of calling her father with the news but he was probably still at school. Chris wouldn't be home from work for another hour. She opened a beer and stood at the window watching two squirrels chase each other across the fork in the branches of the elm tree in the yard and then disappear down the other side.

The letters from the colleges signaled the end to the old life; no doubt, if she went away to school, Chris would sell the house. Though now that Chris was going out with Bud Chaffin, the guy who owned the nursery, she might not be so reluctant to leave East Winston after all. Billie was glad that her mother was finally going out with someone, even though Bud was ten years younger and Billie felt wary about his motives and his interest in Chris. It wasn't only his age that made Billie suspicious but the way he refused to look at her directly when he talked, his cerulean blue eyes reflecting a wall of calm, so that often she felt like she was obstructing his view, that what he was really looking at was taking place beyond her.

It suddenly seemed as if each member of the family had become so involved with their own lives that no one had time to think about anyone else. Joanne had quit her job mid-semester at Berkshire Community and was subletting an apartment on 112th Street on the Upper West

Side in Manhattan. At least that's what Chris had said in response to Billie's questions about whatever was going wrong between her father and his wife.

Mitch refused to talk about it; whenever she slept over he spent most of the time in his room.

"He's going through a bad period," Chris said, more generous with her sympathy than Billie imagined she could ever be.

In Billie's mind, it stood to reason that Chris might at least secretly hate the person who had lured her husband away and be gleeful that both Mitch and Joanne (the shoe on the other foot etc.) were now suffering.

All of Chris's friends were excited that she was finally coming out of her shell and Billie was amazed to find her preening in front of the bathroom mirror, putting on makeup with names like Vanderbilt, Denevue, L'Oreal and Clinique. There was a ring in her voice; often, in mid-sentence, she would burst into giddy laughter. Whatever combination of events, she had managed to cast off her defenses ("just because I've been hurt once doesn't mean it's going to happen again") and begin the process of reinventing her life.

"What do you think?"

Billie, who was still plowing through *Middlemarch*, looked up from the book. Chris was wearing a tight turquoise skirt which zipped up the side, matching turquoise heels with open toes, no stockings, a light blue blouse which buttoned up the front and a turquoise barrette in her hair.

"You look great," Billie said, careful not to show her disapproval at her mother's taste in men. Going out with Bud was a start and possibly it would give her the confidence to know that she was still attractive.

Though Chris had to be at the bank at 8:30 every morning, she often stayed out till one or two. Bud, as part owner of the nursery, had the freedom to come and go as he pleased. Often Billie was awake, reading in bed, or just lying awake with the lights off, unable to fall asleep (she tried masturbating to the fantasy of fucking Eduardo Narcimento—she was lying on her stomach and he was coming at her from behind—but it only made her more wakeful), when Chris returned home.

"Is that you, Mom?"

She could hear her mother's voice; she and Bud were talking in the kitchen. Bud Chaffin lived in the same housing community as Bob Rodgers and Billie assumed that's where they spent their evenings together.

She talked with Eduardo every night on the phone. He asked her to help him with English and she gave him books to read: *The Stranger*, *The Sun Also Rises*, *Madame Bovary*, *Tender is the Night*, *Great Expectations*. And some short stories too, from an anthology she found on her father's shelf: "I'm A Fool," by Sherwood Anderson, "I Stand Here Ironing" by Tillie Olsen, "A Rose for Emily" by Faulkner, Hemingway's "Hills Like White Elephants."

Unlike Howard or Ted, Eduardo made a conscientious attempt to read all the books she recommended. He couldn't understand how Charles Bovary didn't know his wife was sleeping with other men or how Emma herself could be so stupid not to realize Rodolphe had no real feelings for her. Bille reminded him that blindness was one of the book's major themes and pointed out the appearance of the blind beggar at the end.

"I haven't gotten that far," Eduardo confessed.

As the star of the track team, he wasn't permitted out on weekday nights, so they had to be content with seeing each other between classes and after school and on Friday and Saturday nights.

Howard also called almost every night. Annette, apparently, was spending more and more time with Bob Rodgers (Bob's wife had left, finally, and returned to her parents' home in Portland, Maine) and Howard stayed home with Emma and Sara. Billie couldn't understand why Howard didn't go out at least once a week ("if you really wanted to see me, you could hire a babysitter") and why Annette never stayed at home, ever, with the kids.

"Why are you so frightened of her?"

"I'm not frightened. I'm just waiting for the right moment."

It was over, it was almost over. They still met every Friday in the parking lot behind the library. They still drove to the Acorn Acres to make desultory love on the big bed under the framed prints of the Parthenon and the Acropolis. The blue of the Aegean Sea was the color of Eduardo's eyes.

Howard still referred to the future as if he and Billie would eventually live together. Everything depended, as far as he was concerned, on where Billie decided to go to college.

"But what about Emma and Sara?"

Billie never had the feeling that Howard was truly interested in the children and that he wouldn't put up much of a fight if some time in the future a court turned over the custody of Emma and Sara to Annette. She smoothed her skirt over her thighs and walked out into the mid-afternoon light. Howard sat behind the wheel of his Cadillac, smoking a cigarette, brooding.

"Have you been seeing that Spanish guy? Are you sleeping with him?"

Howard always became angry when she didn't want to make love more than once. He assumed her lack of desire had to do with Eduardo Narcimento, that she was lying when she said that she and Eduardo were good friends, nothing more. Sometimes when they separated in the parking lot behind the library he refused to say goodbye, or even look at her.

"I'm tired of your sour moods," she said, slamming the car door. "Why don't you go home to your lovely wife?"

In the evening, after one of these scenes, he called to apologize.

"What are you doing?"

"I'm reading *Middlemarch*."

She told him about the novel, who wrote it ("a woman named George"), hoping that retelling the story would be as boring as actually reading it. She knew, from his silence, that he wasn't even listening.

"So you're not angry anymore?"

"Angry about what?"

"About what happened this afternoon. I just don't like the idea that you're seeing that guy."

"But what about Annette? You don't seem to mind that she sees other people. And for all I know, you and Annette might be sleeping together too."

"I'm not in love with Annette."

"I don't follow you," she said. "You let Annette do whatever she wants. She goes out and fucks other people and you're waiting right there at home—if she ever comes home. But me! If I have a friend, if I even talk to one other person, you start throwing a tantrum. Letting people do what they want, letting them be themselves, that's more my idea of love than trying to possess them."

"Where did you read that?" Howard asked, as if what she learned from books was more a threat than Eduardo himself.

"You're sick," she said. "That's the sickest thing I ever heard. From now on I'm going to see Eduardo as much as I want."

Then she hung up.

*

April 19

Dear Billie,

I do want to know your real name and, no, I didn't mind your letter. The same day yours arrived I received one from my sister. Her name, like your mother's, is Chris, Christina.

She's my oldest sister, I told you about her, the one who took care of me after my mother died.

Your problems with your family do seem simpler than mine but I still sympathize with you. Maybe it's just as hard to have parents as not to have them? And my relationship with my sister confuses me, too, sometimes. I hate her husband—if I had a lot of money I'd pay someone to kill him. Christina hates him too, she loves and hates him at the same time, but she's frightened that he'll murder her if she files for a divorce. And all this despite the fact that my sister is one of the most powerful women in Mexico City, she's on television all the time and her articles are syndicated in newspapers throughout the country.

Everyone knows that her husband is a crook but no one's going to touch him as long as he's married to Christina. For many years I lived with Christina and her husband in a big house with lots of bodyguards and Doberman Pinchers and burglar alarms. A guy with a machine gun in a small tower overlooking the driveway! Just like some scene in "Miami Vice" only my brother-in-law isn't involved in selling drugs—even though he's as sleazy as any of the dealers on that show—but holds a corner of the market for artifacts, pots and statues and bones and little religious ikons, all of which he and his gang looted from some archeological site in the middle of the jungle. He can sell these objects for thousands of dollars each, they were priceless, he literally went into the jungle with pickaxes and chain saws and shovels and bulldozers and returned with truckloads of relics. And no one could stop him or figure out what he was doing since all the cops in the nearby towns were being paid to look the other way. Anyway, I tried to spend as much time as possible away from the house but when I was around, my sister and I would always eat together at the opposite ends of a long dining room table, under chandeliers or with candles, as if we were king and queen in a castle.

My sister dressed up as if our dinner together was a special occasion. She was beautiful but her life with Luis, my brother-in-law, was making her age rapidly. Before she went to bed she always covered her face with hideous creams and lotions to make her look young. When she was younger—when she was your age—she always had the most boyfriends, she could take her pick. Alas, one of her problems is that she's unable to have children. I was like her child, that's what she always said to me.

We sat at the ends of the table and the maid, the house was filled with servants, most of them women, this maid's name was Lavinia, brought us our food. My brother-in-law would force all the servants to have sex with him, he would rape them and threaten them if they ever said anything. Lavinia told me and made me swear never to tell my sister. People in Mexico City are very poor and Lavinia was probably supporting half a dozen people, including her own children, with the money she made working for us. So there was no way she wasn't going to do whatever Luis wanted. I don't know what your image of poverty might be or how you imagine poor people live or what it means to you to go hungry not for a few hours at a time but for weeks or months on end. I can remember living in a shack outside Rio with a thatched roof which leaked on my blankets when I slept.

Some days all I ate was a small plate of rice and beans. That was before my sister became a famous journalist and my cousin a popular singer and before my father died and before I came from Rio to Mexico City and started running. But why am I writing you all this?

The thing I like most about living in a small town is that everyone knows everyone else and that no one's frightened of anyone. People I don't know say hello to me on the street. Everyone is so friendly and helpful and meeting you—this has been important to me, but confusing as well. It would be wonderful to travel to Mexico together. I could show you the Chpultepec Castle and the beautiful murals where Christina used to take me when I was growing up and to University City where I dreamed about going to school before I decided to come here and to Xochmilco, the "floating gardens." I would introduce you to my sister who wouldn't be shocked by the fact that we were traveling together and not married—in this way, her openmindedness, she is different from most people in Mexico—but she would probably be jealous that I loved someone more than her.

(later) It's "waiting for dinner" time and I'm up in my room. This house is noisy. Susan is always playing her radio and Manny and Esta are always arguing about something. At first I thought it would be hard to live in a house with a girl my own age who wasn't part of my family but I think I can honestly say that Susan's become a good friend, almost like a sister, and I feel I can talk to her about almost anything.

(She teases me about you alot but I think she thinks you're "the cat's pajamas"—that's a phrase she taught me

but I'm not sure what it means. It's a good thing, yes?) She wants to talk to me about her parents who are very strict with her and don't approve of her boyfriend. If she comes home 5 minutes late, Manny's all over her and often won't even talk to her the next day. I feel a little weird because I'm grateful to Manny for getting me the scholarship but I think he's treating Susan unfairly and I know it makes her unhappy because she really loves him. The real issue in this household is that Manny thinks Esta is having an affair and literally tortures her about it. I know that when Manny goes out she has mysterious phone conversations but I don't know—and I don't want to know—who she's talking to. Susan is so unhappy. I wish you and she were better friends. I sometimes think I'm the only person she can talk to.

I have a memory of taking a bath with my sister and thinking she was mother. The next time I see you remind me to show you a picture of her.

Till then,

Eduardo

*

Her mother was out with Bud Chaffin almost every night and her father was never home except on weekend afternoons.

"He probably has a girlfriend too," she told Nicky.

"I wish my parents would have lovers."

"I can't imagine it."

"I think they've probably forgotten what to do...."

"But I hate this guy Chaffin. I don't know what my mother sees in him."

"Maybe you're just jealous that he's attracted to her instead of you. I think he's cute."

Billie invented a brief fantasy in the hope of discrediting Bud Chaffin in her mother's eyes. He came to the house when Chris wasn't around and made a pass at Billie. When she resisted he pulled out a knife, pressed it to the side of her neck, and forced her to have oral sex.

"What if I told you I was pregnant?" Nicky asked.

"I don't believe you."

"I'm not asking you to believe me. I'm telling you."

"Then I'd say: who's the lucky father?"

"And I'd say: it's none of your fucking business."

She wanted to tell Nicky about Howard and Eduardo. She wanted to tell her about Whip—how they had met one afternoon in the hardware store after school and had driven in his battered pick up to his room in The Carmel Arms, a boarding house on the East Winston-Carmel Road, and how easy it had been to make love with someone you like and trusted and who you considered a friend but who you weren't in love with.

(We didn't say anything. The room contained a bed with a soft mattress, a small wooden desk with initials carved into the surface, and a mahogany bureau with three drawers. There was a photograph of a young woman with red hair—"my daughter"—tacked to the edge of the oval mirror above the bureau. Whip had a quart of beer and poured out two glasses, tilting the glass so the head wouldn't spill over the rim. It was warm in the room, airless, and

Whip just reached out and began unbuttoning my blouse. I didn't move, except to reach behind me and unfasten my bra. My heart was beating as fast as that first time with Arnie on the beach and I remembered the time I met Whip in the bar with Ted that first night we went out and he got drunk and I kissed him good night in his car. Everything was in slow motion, like a series of still lifes, or slides. His hands reaching up under my skirt to slide my underpants down my legs, his fingers inside me, his mouth between my legs. When we made love, he took my hands and held them together in one of his so that I couldn't reach out and touch him. It was as if my hands were tied above my head. I opened my eyes wide when he did that—no one had ever done anything like that before—and he smiled and said "Don't worry, I'm not going to hurt you" and I felt like saying "You can do what you want, I want you to hurt me," but I didn't, I kept my mouth shut and closed my eyes as tight as I could.)

She wanted to tell Nicky how comfortable she felt when she was getting dressed in front of him, as if she had nothing to hide, no secrets, and how there was no reason to speak, no need to ask "Will I see you again?" and how being in Whip's room was like being outside time or in a parallel dimension where time didn't exist, no thought of Howard or Eduardo or Ted, no thought of her parents or of what the future might bring, how there was nothing but the light through the curtains on her skin as she lay in Whip's arms playing with the hair on his chest, how for the first time in her life she was living in the present.

"I saw Ted in school with that girl," Nicky said.

"She's a sophomore but she looks about twelve."

"I heard she's going to try out for cheerleading."

"Happily I won't be around."

"Do you think they're doing it?"

"Doing what?"

"Don't be cute."

"Why don't you say what you mean. I can't imagine Ted wasting his time if he wasn't fucking her."

She was alone one night taking a bath when she thought she heard footsteps, called out her mother's name though she wasn't sure it was Chris. Chris always slammed the front door as a signal to Billie that she was home, or called up the steps to let her know she was there. It was only eleven o'clock, too early for Chris, who never returned home before midnight when she went out with Bud. The bathroom door was locked. Billie stood up quickly, tied a towel around her breasts and thighs, and cradled the plunger (it was the only feasible weapon) like a rifle in her arms, the water dripping from her legs onto the bathroom tiles.

"Who the fuck is it?" Billie screamed, as the steps grew closer.

But no one answered.

"You should be glad that your mother's so happy."

"I am. But what happens if she decides to marry this guy?"

"Don't worry, you won't be around then either."

"My stepfather. Bud. Mr. Chaffin. What should I call him?"

"I saw your father today."

"Where?"

"In the library. He was with somebody...."

"A she."

"A her. And it wasn't Joanne."

"Anyone we know?"

"I never saw her before in my life but I bet she's a lot younger than Bud Chaffin. Younger than you, maybe."

"Was she pretty?"

"She was tiny, a little mousy. I didn't think that was your father's type."

"One of his students."

"He saw me and said hello, but he didn't introduce us."

"You're definitely not his type," Billie said. "Why should he?"

Her father's house was empty. There was a note on the kitchen table saying he'd be back about eight and that she should make dinner for herself if she wanted. Eduardo was picking her up at 7:30. Mitch and Eduardo had met and seemed to like one another. Eduardo, always curious about other people, had even managed to get Mitch talking about his classes at Berkshire Community and the books he was teaching. Mitch was impressed that Eduardo had been accepted by Columbia, even if it had more to do with his success as an athlete than his work as a student.

Billie hadn't made up her mind where she was going but Barnard was certainly high on her list. Brown was offering more money but Mitch had said that money shouldn't be the main factor and if Billie wanted to go to

New York that was fine with him. Chris, who often talked about moving to Boston, was partial to Brown, which was only an hour away. But ultimately the choice was up to her and right now all she wanted was to go where Eduardo was going. She put on her lipstick, one of the Continuous Color shades which Joanne had left behind, flashed a smile at herself in the bathroom mirror, and went down to the living room to wait for Eduardo.

She wanted to pretend, with Eduardo, that it was really the first time. At least she could sense the way it was different from making love to Ted or Howard or Arnie or Richard or even Whip. She hated them all, she wished she'd never seen any of them.

("If I ever run into him," she told Nicky in response to the news that Arnie Royce had returned to East Winston after a year of lying on the beaches of Southern California, "I'll spit in his face.")

She thought of Ted, she could see his eyes, all the nights on the living room floor at Howard and Annette's. She was wearing the green skirt, Ted's old favorite, the one Joanne had bought her at The Lemon Tree on her last birthday and which Billie had hidden away in the back of the closet (as if hiding something was a way of forgetting, of pretending it didn't exist) after she and Ted split up.

It was only after she zipped it up the back, while waiting for Eduardo to arrive, and was staring at herself in her bedroom mirror that she heard Ted's voice— "don't take it off"—the first night they made love at the Ryan's. The sound of his voice emanated from beneath her skin, as if part of him were locked inside her body.

She smoothed the fabric over her hips and turned in the mirror, remembering the afternoons when she danced for Ted in the upstairs bedroom of his mother's house. She opened the drawer of her bureau and spread her blouse on the bed (the one with the tropical fruit pattern was a favorite but looked better worn loose with pants than with the skirt), trying to decide what to wear.

"You look pretty," Eduardo said, "is that a new skirt?"

She sat in the bucket seat of his white Volvo and watched the back of his hand as he shifted gears. In a car like this, she thought, there's no way you can make love to the driver. As usual, Eduardo was dressed immaculately, as if he'd bought all his clothing especially for this date: a light-blue blazer, a rust-colored denim shirt, a new pair of jeans, white sneakers.

Billie sat as close to him as possible, hoping he'd put his free arm around her shoulders, but he never did. She brushed a strand of hair from in front of her eyes and watched the arrow of the speedometer as it leapt from twenty to fifty to seventy-five as they turned onto the highway (there was the Acorn Acres with the lights reflecting the chemical blue of the rectangular swimming pool and the "No Vacancy" sign with the first "c" missing and the cars lined up outside all the rooms in their little slots including the room where she met every Friday with Howard) leading from East Winston to Pittsfield.

The clouds were coming together on the horizon, moving fast, trailing red and yellow vaporous streams in the wake of the setting sun.

The landscape sped by in a blur of trees and houses, an occasional cow or horse in the middle of a field staring wistfully at its own shadow. The road was straight, there were no other cars, the point of the speedometer was at eighty but it felt like they weren't moving at all. Billie rolled down her window, turned her face to the sky, and closed her eyes.

Unlike Ted, Eduardo always knew exactly where he was going. He called Billie during the week and asked her what she wanted to do over the weekend. He made suggestions, he made plans. He held open the door of the car on the passenger side and waited till she was comfortable before closing it gently. Money, apparently, was no problem, at least she didn't have to worry that it was a problem, and when they were out together he insisted on paying for everything. He paid for her but never made any attempt to do anything but kiss her good night. Unlike most men, he wasn't trying to buy her affection. Billie felt that he took his sense of respect for women to an extreme; he was frightened of doing something that he might have to apologize for afterwards, and as a consequence didn't do anything. "Prudish" was the word Nicky used when Billie talked to her about her relationship with Eduardo, but it was more a kind of ignorance of what desire, for a woman, might be.

He didn't understand that making love wasn't a matter of forcing a woman to do something she didn't want.

She was frightened of being too forward, at least in his eyes, of scaring him off. If he wanted to go to the movies that was fine with her.

They had already seen *The Color Purple*, *Out of Africa*, *The Toxic Avenger* and *Pretty In Pink* on previous dates. Tonight they were going to see *The Money Pit*. It was playing in a theater in a big shopping center on the edge of town. There were six theaters and six movies playing at the same time but the theaters were tiny airless spaces, crowded and filled with a stale smell that resembled the inside of someone's old shoes: didn't anyone clean these places out when the screen went blank and the crowd dispersed? Even Eduardo looked distorted in the fountain of artificial light that spewed forth from the spindly columns surrounding the parking lot like an army of aliens.

They sat in Eduardo's car watching the lines inch forward in front of each of the six ticket windows. Billie saw someone she knew from school and someone who looked familiar but whose name she couldn't remember and there was Debbie Pilute, whom she hadn't seen since the last game of the season, standing next to a guy with pasty white skin, spiked blonde hair, and a black leather vest with the words "Kill For Peace" painted on the back. Debbie was wearing a black leather skirt, black stockings with a large rip in each seam, a black t-shirt with the letter X hand-painted down the front, a gold cross dangling from one ear. The people waiting on line behind Debbie and her friend stood about a yard away and stared at them unabashedly as if they were some side attraction hired by the owners of the movie theater to perform in the parking lot or the carriers of a new disease.

Billie wondered what college Debbie Pilute was going to attend, if any. Billie had decided on Barnard and had even received a letter from Joanne telling her she was welcome to stay with her if she ever wanted to visit New York before September. According to Chris, Joanne's departure had been precipitated by her discovery that Mitch was having an affair with one of his students, but

Billie guarded herself against her mother's interpretation. She couldn't believe that a simple infidelity could destroy a relationship, that her father would risk losing Joanne by sleeping with someone else. She had the feeling from Mitch that the separation wasn't irreversible and that he was expecting her to move back but he wasn't sure exactly when.

The letter from Joanne triggered a stream of new fantasies: Eduardo was going to Columbia, he had a track scholarship, they would both live in the dorms but if they ever wanted to be together they could go to Joanne's apartment when she wasn't there. The apartment, as Joanne described it, was just a studio with a loft, windows looking out over The Hudson River. Billie imagined opening the door of Joanne's apartment with her own key, undressing in front of the icy sunlit windows, and waiting in bed for Eduardo to join her.

Eduardo wanted to go out to eat after the movie, there was a Mexican restaurant in Pittsfield, that's what they usually did after the movies, but this time Billie vetoed the idea and suggested going to the lake. If they went out to eat he would just take her home afterwards, kiss her good night, and that would be it. It was the first night warm enough to actually imagine making love out of doors though Billie wasn't certain that Eduardo knew that's what she had in mind or that the lake was the traditional place where lovers went.

The movie had been horrible (that was her opinion, anyway, though most of the audience, including Eduardo, seemed to love it) and she wanted to salvage some bit of pleasure from their night together. Eduardo was always curious about why Billie liked or disliked something and was especially intrigued by the strength of her opinions.

"I didn't think it was that bad," was his most frequent comment, and Billie often wondered if he felt strongly about anything.

During the movie Billie had rested her head on Eduardo's shoulder and had placed his hand on her knee, holding it in her own hand. She had pulled up her skirt so his fingers were resting on her bare flesh. During the course of the movie his hand slid up beneath her skirt so that it was resting on the top of her thigh. A couple in the row in front of them were necking passionately, oblivious to everything that was going on around them, and Billie hoped they would inspire him to go even further.

The lake was at the end of a dirt road leading from the highway between Pittsfield and East Winston. They parked in a small clearing and sat for awhile looking out at the water. There were no other cars around but it was still early. In recent years, since gangs from nearby Lakeside High School had begun to come on motorcycles to torment their more well-heeled neighbors, the lake had lost its popularity as a place to go and make out.

They were lying on a blanket on the sand, a few feet from the water. The moon was almost full, the tops of the trees outlined by a pale aura. Billie knotted her ankles at the base of Eduardo's spine and placed her hands on the back of his neck.

At first she thought he was going to come as soon as he entered her. He moaned loudly, as if he had a cramp in his side, and began moving fast as if he wanted it to be over as soon as possible.

Billie tensed her whole body in expectation of the moment when he would explode and collapse on top of her and was surprised when he suddenly began to move in regular strokes, neither too slowly nor too fast but with occasional bursts of freneticism interspersed with periods of calmness where the time between strokes seemed to last for minutes and she began to feel if he didn't push against her again she would lose her mind. It was she who was moaning now, while he teased her, holding himself above her, his fingers splayed on either side of the blanket.

"Fuck me," she said, she couldn't help herself, "come inside me, come all the way."

Eduardo removed his shirt and pants but Billie didn't bother to take off her skirt. It was bunched up around her waist and covered with sand. Her blouse was open and every so often he lowered his mouth and kissed one of her breasts.

She heard the waves brush up against the shoreline and a frog in the bushes at the edge of the lake and what sounded like a foghorn from somewhere in the sky but which was probably only the horn of a car. The road circled the lake and an occasional pair of headlights flickered between the tree trunks. Most of the houses bordering the lake were empty during the winter. Billie had heard stories about motorcycle gangs breaking into these houses and using them for parties and for a moment she imagined that the person making love to her had a long scrawny beard and big tattoos of naked women on both his arms and a wide silver belt which scratched her thighs as he pressed against her....

They reversed positions, Billie on top, her skirt floating over Eduardo's legs.

This was the position that Ted always liked the best. Eduardo placed his hands on her hips and steadied her when she began to move too quickly.

Obviously, he had an idea about a way of moving that would give them the maximum amount of pleasure. Billie had to laugh at herself for ever thinking that Eduardo's reluctance to make love was a result of his inexperience. She closed her eyes and dipped her head so that her hair fell across Eduardo's face and thought of Bud Chaffin and what would happen if he ever came by when she was alone....

"What did you do that for?" He had slipped away and moved out from under her.

"No reason. I just want to stop."

"Don't you want to come?"

"I guess so. What about you? Did you come?"

"A lot of times I don't come when I fuck but sometimes I do if you touch me."

"You mean you make love with other guys?"

She avoided the question.

"Do you want me to touch you?" She reached for his cock but he pushed her hand aside.

"Maybe later," he said.

"But it was so nice to make love to you." She felt like crying.

"I've been thinking about it for weeks."

She said, "I thought you were a virgin, but I guess I was wrong."

"I wondered if you were too. But I didn't know. From what Susan told me, very few high school girls are virgins in this country."

"And in your country?" She couldn't believe they were talking, that they had stopped making love, that sex was over.

"Oh, all the girls are virgins until they get married. Almost all the time. Many of them get married very young. By the time they're your age they have two or three kids. If you don't get married by the time you're twenty you might never get married. You're considered old when you're twenty. And some girls are raped by their fathers or uncles and get pregnant and have illegitimate children since abortions are unheard of. Most of these women end up in nuthouses. Or become nuns."

"I'm not a virgin, it's true," she said dreamily. She was lying alongside him, her head on his arm, thinking of the song "Like A Virgin."

"But the others don't count," she said. "And there really haven't been many others. This was like the very first time...."

"What do you mean?"

Billie wasn't certain what she meant. The meaning was in the sound of the words and the way she said them. Yet she felt confused: was this it?

Had they made love? Were they finished? She felt no better than she ever had when she made love to Ted.

"It would embarrass you if I told you what I mean. I'll write you a letter about it."

"It's important for me to know because in a way you are right. I am a virgin. Or was until now."

She wanted to laugh at the seriousness of his voice and began to hate him for not wanting to make love to her again. Maybe crying out, begging him to keep fucking her, something she had never done before, had frightened him.

"I don't believe it," she said. "I never slept with a virgin but my friend Nicky has and she told me what that was like. I'm afraid you don't fit the description. You're too good."

"I've made love before," his voice had gone cold, "but only to one other person."

"Then you're not a virgin."

She wanted to ask "who"—who was your lover?—but assumed that it would just be the name of someone she didn't know and that consequently there was no point in even telling her. Maybe he went to a prostitute or maybe he didn't remember his lover's name the same way Billie had forgotten Arnie's last name for these two years. It was natural, when you regretted doing something, to try to block it out, to pretend it didn't happen.

From Eduardo's tone she sensed something was wrong. She felt her desire for him subsiding in trepidation of what he was about to say, but when he finally blurted out "Don't you want to know who?" she went along with it, said "Sure, if it's so important to you," even though she didn't really care. Then he rolled away from her so that all she could see was the outline of his back in the moonlight, his shoulder a small hill outlined against the sky.

She didn't realize he was crying. He pressed the edge of the blanket against his face to muffle the sound of his voice.

"It's my sister."

"What did you say?"

"My sister and I were lovers. That's why I'm so scared now. I don't know why but I can't stop thinking about her."

He buried his face in his hands and cried for half a minute. In the distance she could hear the rumble of a motorcycle on the other side of the lake. Or maybe it was just a car with a faulty muffler?

"I'm so sorry," he said. "Say something to me. Tell me you understand. I know I need help."

(I wanted to reach out and touch his shoulder and comfort him but I didn't do anything. I wanted to say "it doesn't matter" or "it won't change anything" but the only words that came into my head were "Oh shit, not again." At first I couldn't believe what he was saying and I made him repeat it: my sister and I were lovers, my sister and I were lovers. It infuriated me that he had ruined everything just because of that. Really, who cares anyway? Something happens in the past but you don't hold onto it and let it fuck up everything that takes place later. What bothered me wasn't that he'd slept with his sister but that he told me about it, that

he'd let it get to him to the extent that he couldn't make love to me, that he wouldn't continue what he started so sweetly on the beach where two years before I lost my virginity with Arnie Royce, then a week later with Richard, then almost a year and a half later with Ted. And it all came back: the sad feeling of lying next to Ted after we made love and wondering why he didn't touch me and why he only wanted to make love when I wore a certain skirt and why he cared more about drinking beer than he did about me. And I thought of the afternoons up in his room when his mother wasn't home. He's lying back on the bed and I'm spinning around the room, singing along to the music on the tape deck. It's not that I want to suffer but I'm willing to do almost anything in order to be loved. "Lift your skirt," "take off your blouse," "turn around"—a feeling of humility washes over my head like a wave, littering the beach with dead fish. I'm alone on the shore, on an island, looking out at the horizon. I'm waiting for a boat to stop and take me aboard, take me away from here. I imagine the sailors staring at me through their binoculars. I feel like a siren sitting on a rock beckoning the sailors to their ultimate doom. I want to tell all those young men in their white suits that I'll make love to each of them. And then I'm back in the bed in the motel with Howard, lying next to him as he complains about Annette and how he's going to leave her, it's just a matter of waiting for the right moment. How often I've heard that! After Ted, I know I need something more, that I want to give myself to another person but I know that giving only works if the other person considers your needs as well. Only a crazy person keeps giving without getting anything in return. A crazy person, a saint. I have to fight against the part of me that wants to be a slave, your devoted servant. And I realize, now, that there's almost nothing you can do to heal the wounds and scars of the past without losing a sense of your own being, that it isn't your job to shield a person from the sickness of a world where people are starving on the streets and whole countries of children are going hungry while men in 3-piece suits and expensive cigars allocate billions of dollars to build weapons. And that's just part of it, as if growing up and living inside one's own personal dilemmas wasn't enough. How can you aspire to clarity and simplicity when everyone's lives are so complicated? You want to get back to that time before you had to deal with other people's problems, before you had hair on your legs, before you had to worry about blood pouring out of your body every month, before the love of other people was the only thing that mattered. Look at poor Jake Barnes, in The Sun Also Rises, *who can't make love to anyone, or Meursault, in* The Stranger, *who would make love to anyone, indiscriminately, who didn't believe in love, who cared for nothing but his own comfort. I've had many lovers since that year, my senior year in high school, both men and women, and it's always the same: when someone begins telling me their story I swallow hard, I steady myself, and when they're finished they look at me and say: "What a good listener you are!" They love me because I pay so much attention to them. I ask them questions. I get them to try to understand what happened in the past to make them feel the way they do.*

"You'd make a good therapist," my girlfriend Peggy tells me. Part of me wants to close my ears: I don't want to hear any of it.

And when it's my turn to tell the story, I just smile and shake my head. They have to pry it out of me! And so I tell them about the year my parents split up and how I would shuffle back and forth between their houses and how before that I used to lie awake listening to them fight and how my father used to stay out late and my mother would accuse him of having lovers and how finally he left her for another woman and eventually remarried and how she, his second wife, eventually left him for the same reason. And I'll talk about how I lost my virginity in my sophomore year in high school and how the guy wouldn't even talk to me afterwards and how the next week I made love with his best friend and how he wouldn't talk to me either and how I stopped going out with anyone for over a year after that, I didn't trust anyone until I met Ted. And then I'd describe Ted: his drinking, his refusal to touch me, his insistence that I wear a specific article of clothing when we made love, the green skirt with the yellow flowers. I try to understand why it all happened this way, I have a little distance now, I can look back and laugh a bit since what happened to me was so less horrible than the experiences of others: my parents, after all, were still alive, I should be thankful for that, I was successful in school—there were doors open to me, not to use a cliché, but that's what everyone always said, options, choices, things to do, I should count my blessings. I would laugh, then, because I was embarrassed to talk so much about myself, and I would tell whoever was listening (were they really interested?) about Howard, the married man, the man who had hired me to babysit for his children, how once a week we drove to a motel room and made love and how every time I slept with someone I was under the illusion that I was in love with this person and how this married man wanted to leave his wife and children and live with me, at least that's what he said, but really, both he and Ted were two of the unhappiest people I've ever met and maybe they liked me because they saw me as a person who had somehow kept herself immune from the insidious web of misery that makes it impossible for most people to experience anything in a genuine way. If only they knew how many ways I devised to protect myself! I can do something to change the world but I can't save you from yourself. I don't want to. I look at Eduardo and see a person standing alone at the crossroads where past, present, future and all the possibilities intersect, not knowing whether to turn left, right, just go straight or possibly step backwards and return to where he came from, and that the person who just made love to me, who tried to, who was too frightened to make love because of something that had happened to him when he was younger, is like a fragment of a whole person who exits now as a shadow of some future being. And I'll never know that person. Maybe we'll meet some day, maybe Ted and I will meet in some future life as well, maybe we'll all meet eventually and recognize our true faces. But meanwhile I'm going to proceed down my own path and though it's sad to separate myself from all the people in my past I hope that in the short time we were together each of us learned something from one another that will benefit not only ourselves but our future lovers as well. And what's saddest of all is that now I have to put my love for Eduardo to one side, discard it like an old rag, toss it overboard into the deep. Because even though I love him I have no inclination to cast off my own dreams and devote myself to helping him realize his own; and all I can do, if even that, since I've never met anyone who's slept with his sister before, is to point out some way in which he can help himself, then disappear.)

They were in the car, backing out of the clearing, the aura from the headlights swerving over the tops of the bushes and trees. Billie sat as far from him as possible, the moonlight pouring in through the windshield onto her lap. She flattened the skirt over her knees and buried her face in her hands, falling forward against the dashboard as the car hit a rock.

"I'm sorry," Eduardo said. He was no longer crying, but his voice was like a machine, like he had memorized a "How to learn English" tape and was reciting it back to her.

"I thought you would understand. I didn't mean to upset you. I told you about my sister so that you'd know me better. Why do you think I stopped myself from having sex with you all these months? Do you think I didn't want to touch you? Why do you think I stopped tonight? I can't ignore what happened with my sister, I can't walk around with this secret.

"It's better to tell you now than wait until later so you can't accuse me of hiding anything. Of not being open. It wouldn't have been fair to make love and not tell you.

"Didn't you once say that you wanted me to tell you everything I was thinking? Well here it is. My sister didn't force me to do something I didn't want to do and in a way it always seemed like the most natural thing in the world. The first time, I was thirteen, and taking a bath in the big house. She came and sat at the edge of the tub, smoking a cigarette, in a red nightgown, and told me how unhappy she was, how Luis, her husband, the guy I wrote to you about, refused to touch her. I knew even then that Luis slept with all the servants and that a few of them had even become pregnant and given birth to his children and that the trouble between my sister and Luis started when he realized she couldn't have children.

"I didn't want to hear what she had to say any more than you want to hear this now but that knowledge made me feel closer to her, made me want to help her even more. And one way of helping was by reaching out and taking her hand. We'd always been affectionate with one another, hugging and holding hands, so it didn't seem wrong to try to comfort her in this way. And once we touched each other it was like all the feelings we shared from living together in a kind of conspiracy—not only against Luis but our parents and all the servants—came flying to the surface full speed.

"In some ways, it was all very innocent, we were like children again and when it was over we'd kiss chastely, like brother and sister, which is what we were, and I'd return to my room. In all that time we never spent a whole night together and no one discovered us when we were making love. Christina always suspected that one of the maids was spying on her but she never knew for certain. We liked to lie in bed and reminisce about our childhood, our parents, we always laughed a lot about everything, even the times when we were living in poverty.

"When I came here, when I left for what we both knew might be an eternity apart from one another, she made me promise never to tell anyone. But I know she probably realized this moment would occur, that I'd meet someone I felt strongly about, it was inevitable, and that I'd want to tell everything....

"I remember when we were poor and living in Sao Paolo we used to keep chickens behind the house and Christina and I would take care of them, she showed me how, and that's when we became friends. We woke at dawn and carried the feed to the shed behind the small shack where we lived, both of us in the same room, and she showed me how to wring the necks of the chickens so that they wouldn't bleed over the feathers. We had names for those chickens: Donna and Rosa and Martha and Delilah. Those were the hens.

"I remember them sitting meditatively on their nests when we came at dawn and the way the shed smelled during the summer as if someone had coated the walls with sour milk and how all the neighbors complained that we had to get rid of the shed or at least clean it out every day. We tried to clean it but the smell never went away. That was a peaceful time when my mother was still alive and my father wasn't angry twenty-four hours a day.

"After she died he used to beat Christina and I tried to protect her by striking back at him. I was only eight at the time and he would end up beating me too. He would get drunk and come into our room, and try to get into bed with Christina. That's why she ran away but before she left she promised she would send for me as soon as she found a place to live. She went to Mexico City and enrolled at the university and met Luis who was wealthy and had a big house and was willing to support her while she was in school. And when she finished school she got a job at the newspaper....

"I've never told anyone about this. I still want to see you when we go to New York. Our lives are changing. What difference does any of this make now?

"I love you," Eduardo said. "I want to tell you everything."

"But when you were with her—was it like us?"

There was no *us*. She had used the word incorrectly. She had spoken just to fill up some kind of space that threatened to engulf them if she didn't say anything. They had existed together for this one period of time and now it was over. She wished he hadn't told her about his sister. They had begun making love on the sand and then they had stopped.

Billie was sick of secrets, of doing things which she couldn't talk about freely with other people. She was tired of getting caught up in the spiderweb of someone else's problems even though it seemed that was the only way to get to know another person. Maybe happiness without problems was an illusion, a myth, and that in order to get along you had to accept another person's fears and hungers, all the demons of the past, as if they were as real as your own.

"She was sitting on the side of the tub and we were reminiscing about how we used to take baths together when we were kids. 'Remember how I used to touch you there,' she said, and we both started laughing."

Once he started talking about the past he didn't want to shut up. In this sense, Eduardo was like Billie's mother or Howard. Or anyone. And he didn't even realize how pathetic he sounded.

Billie held her head between her hands and covered her ears. *(I'll call up Barnard and tell them I'm not going. I can always reapply to Smith or Brown. There's still time. If there's any problem I can go to the local college here for a year and then transfer somewhere else.)*

She wanted to be back in her room, either at Mitch's house or at her mother's, back in a world where all the voices in her head were her own. What she needed was the feeling of familiarity that came from being alone for long periods of time. This is me, she would say to herself, staring at the hair on her arm, and a voice in her head would answer, yes, this is you, this is who you are. You're alive right now, the voice would remind her, reassuringly.

It always seemed odd to Billie to be alive with the knowledge that you were going to have to die some day. She couldn't understand why being aware of death to such an extent didn't exempt you from dying. The feeling of vulnerability which accompanied the knowledge of death was as close to what happened when you fell in love as anything else. Love had a life of its own, and could die as well, feelings might be trampled upon or ignored, the end could come quickly or unexpectedly or it could be a long drawn out demise, with all the pain and heartbreak that accompanied the death of the body.

That Friday she met Howard in the parking lot behind the library, just like always. Her plan was to tell him she didn't want to see him again. He was late, and she waited in the front seat of the Cadillac, rehearsing what she was going to say. She was wearing a tight sleeveless blouse, jeans and sandals, blue triangles dangling from her ears. The last time they talked on the phone, a few nights ago, Howard had told her that Annette was definitely planning to leave and go off with Bob Rodgers. And that she was taking the kids too.

"That means we're free," he had said, almost in the same breath as telling her that he was going to live separately from his children, "to do what we want."

He assumed that after Annette moved out Billie would move in with him.

"You can go to Pittsfield Community for a year," this was the college where her father worked, "while I wind up business here."

He came down the back steps of the library and Billie could tell that he was angry but from his look she couldn't figure out whether it was because of something she had done. He slammed the door of the car and began fishing in his trouser pockets for the keys and then slammed his palm on the wide ledge above the dashboard.

"I left the fucking keys upstairs," he said, glaring at her as if it were her fault he was so distracted.

She'd seen Howard upset before but never like this and it occurred to her that she might be better off writing him a letter instead of confronting him face to face. Given his present state of mind who knows what he might do. Most times, when he was in a bad mood, he acted sullen or just ignored her. He would pout like a young child or turn on her for no reason. She had to beg him to tell her what was bothering him. Mostly, what was bothering him was her "friendship" with Eduardo, but he had too much pride to admit that he was jealous.

"It's Eduardo again, isn't it?" she would say, the accusation making him even angrier.

How dare she tell him what he was feeling. And why he was feeling it. His anger had nothing to do with Eduardo.

"What makes you think I'm jealous of that asshole?"

Luckily, his bad moods never lasted too long, and with a little affection she was usually able to coax him out of the darkness.

"Come here, sit closer to me, you're too far away."

She slid across the vinyl and he put his arm around her shoulders and covered her breasts with the palm of his hand.

"Kind of drunk out today, aren't we?"

He tried to massage her nipple with his palm but she pushed his hand away.

"You know I never drink in the afternoon. I'm just happy Annette finally split. I want to celebrate."

"Where did she go?"

"Where do you think she went?"

He sang the words back at her as if she were demented for even asking.

"Listen Howard, stop treating me like a child. When I ask something just answer me. And get your hand...."

She was tired of being touched by men whenever they felt like it. When she wanted them to touch her they weren't interested. The only reason she was even going to see him was out of respect for a feeling they had once shared.

Out of respect for herself, really, since she could barely remember the person who had looked forward with anticipation and excitement to her Friday afternoons with Howard at the motel, who had sat in her room at her mother's waiting for him to call.

"She wants a divorce."

"I think that's great for you. Really. I think you'll be a lot happier if you get away from her."

He placed his hand along the top of her thigh.

"Turn the station, will you? I don't like this song."

He parked outside their room at the Acorn Acres. It was a few minutes past noon and the blue Cadillac was the only car in the parking area.

"I've been making plans," Howard said, "for you, for me—for both of us."

He unlocked the door, took off his jacket, hung it in the closet and went to the bathroom, whistling and singing to himself, slamming the door shut behind him.

Billie sat on the edge of the bed and decided that when he got out of the bathroom she would tell him it was over. The way he was acting—angry one minute, happy the next—was frightening, and the sooner she told him and left the better off she would be.

She'd spent the week forcing herself to read *Middlemarch* and trying to adjust to her new life: she would go away to school, her mother would marry Bud Chaffin, her father would live by himself and have affairs with all his students.

Eduardo Narcimento called every night but Billie refused to speak to him. Both Eduardo and Howard, she repeated to herself, were part of her past now. All that she had to do was get through the summer. Nicky had told her that she could get a summer job at Caldwell's Supermarket if she wanted and that might be a good idea so she could have some extra money when she went away to college in the fall, even though working as a cashier meant she'd be open target for all the people she wanted to avoid, not only Eduardo and Howard but Arnie Royce as well, and who would find the slightest pretense to confront her at her job. They would pass notes over the counter: I want to see you, please call me. I'll kill myself if I don't see you again.

She heard the water running in the bathroom and spied a bee at the window but couldn't tell whether it was in the room or behind the screen.

She stared at the print of the Acropolis in its imitation wooden frame on the wall above the bed and imagined herself walking around the ruins with a man who was neither Howard nor Eduardo nor Ted but someone she'd just met, a Greek man with long tan legs who took her photograph posing in front of the stones. She was the perfect advertisement. You can walk through these ruins and think of how much the world has changed but here is one place where "forever" has some meaning.

"I'm going to New York next week and I want you to come with me."

"What for?"

"I have to see a client. I'm going to stay at this big hotel uptown, the Park Sheraton. We'll have a ball. We don't have to worry about anything any more. Annette is out of the picture completely. I can just see the look on her face when I tell her that we're going away together. You can come with me and walk around the city while I'm at work"—he was trying to impress her—"and at night we can go see a show. I can get tickets, front row seats. Anything you want to see."

He sat in a green chair, his shirt unbuttoned to his waist, the sleeves rolled up to the elbows. His arms were thin and covered with a down of blonde hair. He hardly ate or slept anymore and Billie was often surprised, given the turmoil in his household, that he could still function at his job, a job which involved giving reassurance and a sense of authority to the people he worked for. No doubt the story about the client in New York was a fabrication, a test to see how she would respond.

"Listen, Howard, I have something to tell you. We have to stop. We can't see each other anymore. I'm going to New York in the fall and I want to spend the summer working and studying. I think it's good that you and Annette aren't living together, but I'm not the one—I'm not the person for you. I want to go to school and read books and meet people my own age. You don't even like to read. I want to see you," this was a lie, "but just as friends."

She couldn't tell from his expression whether he had even heard her and if he did how the words had registered. He was looking past her at the print of the Acropolis and at the flowers embroidered on the curtains which covered the room's only window. It was a small room, claustrophobic, and her words filled all the blank spaces in the air.

"I wish I had a drink," Howard said.

They had had good times together, right here in this room. He would go to the bathroom and she would undress and get into bed. The pool of blue light in the print of the Acropolis reflected a clear empty space in her head. She would climb on top of him so that she was eye level with the print and move slowly in a way she had learned from being with Ted. Slowly, and in control, in the dream-like light drifting through the half-closed blinds, behind which the snow was falling in shifting lines across the field behind the motel, over the hills and the tops of the houses, the shadows of their bodies bobbing up and down in the winter light.

"Anything you want," he said. "We could go to a concert, just tell me what you want to see. I can hire a truck and you can move all your stuff over to my house. I'm already making plans to move to New York in the fall too so we can live there together and you can go to school. I'm sick of being a lawyer, I might go back to school myself. Every few weeks we can come back here and see the kids or they can come and stay with us in New York. We can hire a live-in babysitter.

"Annette doesn't care about the kids and there's not enough room for them where she's living anyway. And I don't think her boyfriend is too keen about living with them either."

And then, with only the slightest pause, and as if the train he was riding had suddenly derailed: "Take off my shoes."

"What did you say?"

"I want you to take off my shoes. And socks. Right now."

"Didn't you hear what I said? It's over. I don't want to make love to you anymore. I didn't come here to sleep with you, just to tell you that it's over."

"It's that guy, Eduardo what's his name, you've been seeing him again."

"I'm not seeing him, you're wrong, that isn't the reason. This doesn't have to do with him. It's you. I'm not interested in anyone. Not him, not you."

"I want you to take off my shoes and then take off all your clothing and get into bed."

"You're crazy. What makes you think you can tell me what to do? You can take off your shoes yourself and get into bed and do whatever you want. I'm leaving."

"You're not going anywhere."

He pushed her backwards onto the bed, holding her by the wrists and pressing the weight of his body against her. He tried to kiss her but she twisted her face to one side.

"Howard, get off me, you're acting like an idiot."

He pressed harder, wedging his knee between her legs. He let go of one of her hands and moved it to her waist, to open the buttons on her pants, and when he did Billie raked her nails along his cheek and grabbed his hair.

"Get off!"

He slapped her hard, once, and then again, as if she were a doll, limp, and he was taking out all his anger on this inanimate object, and then a third time with his fist, spinning her head from side to side.

He raised his arm to hit her again and then stopped.

"I didn't mean to hurt you," he said, rolling away from her, covering his face with his hands.

She took her shoulder bag from the top of a small mahogany bureau and all in one brief moment and without looking back opened the door and stepped outside. She ran past his car down the gravel driveway, past the motel office, towards the road, feeling her face swell where he hit her, the front of her blouse covered with blood.

It was a hot afternoon in early May, summer was in the air, and splinters of tar were rippling in the heat along the edge of the highway.

She stood on the road, almost in the line of traffic, and began waving, frightened that Howard would come running after her and try to drag her back to the room. Her lip was cut, her nose was bleeding, there was a bruise over her right eye. The first car that passed swerved to avoid hitting her and the driver, a man of about Howard's age, alone in his car, shouted something that sounded like "You bitch!" through the open window.

She looked back up the hill and saw Howard at the door of the motel room, arms crossed, tense, staring down at her. Across the road, a woman in shorts and a halter was wheeling a stroller towards the entrance of a new fast food restaurant, the multi-colored pennants hanging listless from the branches of the trees: there was no wind.

Billie wished that Ted would drive by, in his old Plymouth with the beer cans in the back seat, and take her away from here. She remembered the stale odor of his car, the scotch cooler under the dashboard, the overflowing ashtray, the frayed upholstery. It was reassuring to think of him driving around somewhere, right at this moment, a beer can wedged between his knees, just like always. At least once a day Billie thought of calling and asking him if he wanted to go out for a beer, just to talk, but she always lost her nerve. He had a new friend now, a tall thin-waisted girl named Vicki who had a black mole near the corner of her mouth. Billie often saw them at school, holding hands in between classes as they walked silently through the halls. Billie imagined making love to Ted one last time in the back of his car. She wanted the chance to tell him she was sorry for what had happened, that she had made a mistake. "I should have been more patient," she would say, placing his hand on her breast.

She would wear the skirt with the animals on it, a skirt he had never seen. She assumed she had done something to hurt his feelings, something unforgivable, but it just wasn't true.

1984-85
Lake Buel, MA—Brooklyn, NY

Lewis Warsh is the author of two novels, *Agnes & Sally* and *A Free Man*, two books of stories, *Money Under the Table* and *Touch of the Whip*, and numerous books of poems, including *The Origin of the World* and *Avenue of Escape*. His most recent books are *Debtor's Prison*, a book-length poem in collaboration with video artist Julie Harrison, and *The Angel Hair Anthology*, co-edited with Anne Waldman. He has received grants for his fiction and poetry from the National Endowment for the Arts, the New York Foundation for the Arts and The Fund for Poetry. In 1994 he received the James Shestack award from The American Poetry Review. He is editor and publisher of United Artists Books and has taught at SUNY Albany, The New School, Naropa University and The Poetry Project. He is presently on the faculty of Long Island University in Brooklyn.

www.ingramcontent.com/pod-product-compliance
Lightning Source LLC
Chambersburg PA
CBHW011224190726
48287CB00008B/2733

* 9 7 8 1 8 8 1 4 7 1 7 8 3 *